Elliott Coues, Charles Larpenteur

Forty Years a Fur Trader on the Upper Missouri

The Personal Narrative of Charles Larpenteur, 1833-1872

Elliott Coues, Charles Larpenteur

Forty Years a Fur Trader on the Upper Missouri
The Personal Narrative of Charles Larpenteur, 1833-1872

ISBN/EAN: 9783744662567

Printed in Europe, USA, Canada, Australia, Japan

Cover: Foto ©Andreas Hilbeck / pixelio.de

More available books at **www.hansebooks.com**

FORTY YEARS A FUR TRADER

ON THE

UPPER MISSOURI

THE PERSONAL NARRATIVE

OF

CHARLES LARPENTEUR

1833-1872

EDITED, WITH MANY CRITICAL NOTES,

BY

ELLIOTT COUES

MAPS, VIEWS, AND PORTRAITS

IN TWO VOLUMES

VOL. II

NEW YORK

FRANCIS P. HARPER

1898

CONTENTS.

CHAPTER XIX.

(1866–72.)

On and After the Peace Commission.

CHAPTER XX.

CHAPTER XXI.

LIST OF ILLUSTRATIONS.

VOL. II.

CHAPTER XIII.

(1846-47.)

FORT LOUIS AND THENCE TO ST. LOUIS.

EARLY in the spring [of 1846] Mr. McKenzie left on a Mackinaw boat for St. Louis. Nothing of importance took place after his departure until the Company's steamer again arrived, at its usual time, Mr. Honoré Picotte in charge. Mr. Culbertson, who went up a previous summer [in 1844], had burned down Fort Chardon, and gone on with his outfit, according to understanding, to build another post.[1] He had selected, for that purpose, a site five or six miles above Benton, on the south side of the Missouri, named it Fort Louis, and left Mr. Clark in charge. From what motive I cannot say, Mr. Picotte wanted him removed, and on that account arranged with me to go up with the outfit and take charge. I was then

[1] We thus learn that the end of Fort Chardon, near Judith river, and the beginning of Fort Louis, on the Missouri above the future Benton, were almost simultaneous, in the summer of 1844.

getting $600 a year, which he increased to $700. On the 8th of July [1846] I found myself on board a keel boat called the Bear, with 30 men on shore, the tow cord on their shoulders, going at the rate of about 1½ mile an hour, with upward of 800 miles [2] before us. On board were one steersman, two bowsmen, two cooks, and one hunter, who had two men with him and three horses. The boat was well rigged for sailing in case of fair wind, and supplied with sweeps and poles. Though we started at the rate I have said, few know what slow progress is made in such navigation. The banks of the Missouri are lined with thick rosebushes and bull-berry bushes,[3] which are thorny, and sometimes attain the height of 12 feet. Such thickets being impenetrable, men must be sent ahead of the cordelle men, as those who tow the boat are called, to prepare a path for them. Besides this, snags and other incumbrances must be chopped down to clear the cordelle, poling is always slow work, and there are rapids to be overcome, of which I will speak when we reach them. It takes Canadian French

[2] By no means so far as this—the distance may have been called 800 m., but river miles in those days were calculated for the traders by the steamboat men, who stretched to the utmost the mileage by which they were paid for transportation. Fort Louis was actually about 530 m. by the Missouri above the mouth of the Yellowstone, and about 375 by the overland trail.

[3] Otherwise the buffalo berry, *Shepherdia argentea*.

boys to do all this, on meat alone, or only lyed corn, when meat cannot be obtained.

At this slow rate we finally reached a place called Amell's island,[4] a little below the [Picotte's] rapids, where I stopped to make a Mackinaw boat to lighter up the rapids, and also to enable me to keep on to Fort Louis, as the river was very low. A few days after I commenced my boat two men on horseback appeared on the opposite shore. They were sent for and on landing informed us that Harvey had arrived at the mouth of the Yellowstone with a large steamer in opposition, and was making a Mackinaw boat to go up to trade with the Blackfeet. Those men had been sent with a letter to me, requesting me to send them on post-haste to Fort Louis with a letter to Mr. Clark to engage all such freemen as he thought might be of service to Harvey. They were dispatched immediately, and a few days afterward Mr. Clark unexpectedly made his appearance. As I had not sent his

[4] See Lewis and Clark, ed. of 1893, p. 324, for position of this island, and many variants of the personal name by which it afterward became known. It is most frequently Armel and Emil's island on modern maps. The rapids above, which Larpenteur mentions, are Picotte's and several others. Emil's island is 56 river-miles above the mouth of the Musselshell ; it is now 1½ m. long, with its head ½ a m. below present Emil's creek ; which latter is the South Mountain creek of Lewis and Clark, who mention but do not name an island, 2 m. below their South Mountain creek, thus corresponding closely with Emil's, if not the same.

letters, he thought that I was coming to take the charge, and that he would have to serve under me; and after reading his letter from the Company, observed that he would not have served under me had he been ordered to remain, for the reason that he had been a long time with the Blackfeet and thought himself entitled to the charge during the absence of the owner.   This Mr. Clark [5] had been educated at West Point, and was extremely punctilious.   The next day he started back to Fort Louis.

[5] " A Sketch of the Early Life of Malcolm Clark," by his sister, Mrs. Charlotte Ouisconsin Van Cleve, of St. Paul, Minn., occupies Cont. Mont. Hist. Soc. i, 1876, pp. 90–98. He was the son of Lieutenant Nathan Clark, 5th U. S. Infantry, and was born at Fort Wayne, Ind., July 22, 1817. He entered West Point Academy at seventeen, but never graduated, in consequence of some boyish quarrel which was followed by a challenge to fight a duel, a fracas, a court-martial, and his dismissal from the corps of cadets. He went to Texas, served in the Texan army, returned to Cincinnati, and when he was 24 years of age received his appointment to the A. F. Co.

"Sketch of Malcolm Clarke [sic], a Corporate Member of the Historical Society of Montana, by Helen P. Clarke." his daughter, occupies pp. 255–268 of the Society's Contributions, ii, 1896, with portrait opp. p. 329. This article is rather filial than strictly biographical. It appears that Clark came into the country in 1841, made his reputation in the fur trade, and finally settled as a stock-raiser with his family on a ranch in Little Prickly Pear Cañon, Lewis and Clark Co., Mont., in 1864. His first wife, Miss Clarke's mother, was the daughter of an Indian chief; his second was of mixed blood. He acquired two Indian names, White Lodge Pole and Four Bears. He was murdered by two

MALCOLM CLARK.
From only known photograph, in the Montana Historical Society.
(Date Unknown.)

In about a week my boat was finished, we were under way again, and soon came to the rapids. Our lightener did not avail us much, for the river was so low that both boats had to be completely unloaded, and the goods to be carried 400 or 500 yards over the rapids, on the men's backs. The boats were pried over by main force, after clearing the channel of rocks; but this was done with the intention of throwing those rocks back into the channel, so as not to let Harvey overtake us.

Under such slow progress I reached Fort Louis 70

Piegans at or near his home, Aug. 17, 1869, and buried in a spot which was in 1877 on the ranch of Hon. John Fergus. As to the spelling of his name, his daughter uses the *e*, his father did not, and I have never seen his autograph.

To the foregoing sketch is appended an editorial note upon General W. T. Sherman's visit to the grave in 1877: "After supper the General strolled about the place and discovered a grave near by, which he proceeded to investigate. Upon returning to the ranche he mentioned the occurrence and asked a number of questions in order to fix with certainty the personality of the dead, who was none other than Malcolm Clarke, the subject of this sketch; of whom General Sherman said, in substance: that he well remembered Malcolm Clarke, who had been a fellow-cadet with him at West Point and a great favorite there, whom he had there known as a remarkably bright, open-hearted, and high-spirited young man, and for whom he had always prophesied a brilliant future; . . and, finally, that he had lost all trace of his schoolmate since their life at West Point until the discovery by him of the sepulchre among the solitudes of the Rocky Mountains.—W. E. S."

days after my departure from Union.   But I must re-
mark that I had great sport hunting.   The points
above Milk river being cleaner of rubbish than those
below, I commenced my hunt from that river, and the
boat was so slow that I had plenty of time.   I killed
35 deer and 15 elk.   On arrival at Fort Louis I met
with Father De Smet,[6] who was again on his return

[6] This lucky statement enables us to check Larpenteur's
chronology with precision.   The year is 1846.   Reference to De
Smet's Oregon Missions and Travels over the Rocky Mountains
in 1845-46, orig. ed. pub. 1847, p. 307, shows that on Aug. 16,
1846, he left the Bitterroot valley at Hellgate.   Having passed
by way of rivers he calls Cart and Arrowstone to the Jefferson,
he descended the latter to the Madison and Gallatin, went up the
latter and through Bozeman Pass to the Yellowstone, at present
Livingston; passed thence over to some headwaters of the Musselshell, and was camped on Judith river Sept. 13.   On the 18th he
writes, p. 325: " A chief, just arrived, informs us that Black-Feet
of different tribes are assembling in the neighborhood of *Fort
Lewis* to receive their annual supplies, and that the traders who
bring up the goods are distant only three days' journey, with three
large canoes (Mackinaw boats)."   These traders were of course
Larpenteur and his party, then nearing Fort Louis, which De
Smet reached Sept. 24, p. 331.   " The gates were thrown open.   We
received a hearty welcome from every white man in the Fort; the
bourgeois being absent, soon returned, to add by their kindness
and politeness to the warm reception we had already received at
the hands of their tenants."   His companion, Father N. Point,
remained with the Blackfeet here; De Smet departed from Fort
Louis on the 28th; reached Fort Union Oct. 11; left 15th, and
continued down the Missouri to Westport, Mo., Nov. 28, whence
he went by stage to St. Louis, where his next letter is dated Jan.
10, 1847.

from the Columbia to the States.   In about three
days Clark left in a skiff with two men, and then I remained in full charge.   The fort was a good one, well
arranged for the time which had been spent on it.   I
was pleased, and getting along so finely that, had my
family been with me, I should have been perfectly contented; but I had left them at Union.

One fine Indian summer day, about the last of
October [1846], Mr. Clark unexpectedly made his re-
appearance, having received orders at Fort Pierre to
return to Fort Louis, and take charge.   I felt morti-
fied at having my charge taken away from me, and
not even receiving the scrape of a pen from any one.
Feeling myself slighted and remembering what Clark
had said to me in regard to his charge of forts, I
remarked that I supposed he would be willing to
admit that the rule should work both ways.   " I am
not willing to serve under you," I said; " I have been
in this Company's service ten years longer than you
have, and I think that ought to entitle me to a charge
—or, at all events, to justify me in not serving under
you.   So I am going to Fort Union."   Upon which
he remarked that he had nothing to say in the matter,
and if I made up my mind to go, he was willing to
supply me with the means for my trip.

All the men were displeased with the way I had
been treated, and angry to see Clark in charge; for

they disliked him as much as they had Harvey. They proposed my remaining in charge, and assured me they would see me through all right, if I would say the word. But I thanked them, and the second day after Clark's arrival I left on horseback with a first-rate guide named Joseph Howard, one of the oldest hands. Our journey was a pleasant one, but with nothing worth mentioning, and on the 15th of November [1846] we reached Fort Union.

My reception by Mr. James Kipp, who was in charge at the time, was rather cool—" Well, Larpenteur, what brings you down here? " On my relating to him the circumstances, said he, " I am sorry for all that, but I have nothing to do with it. Mr. Picotte engaged you, this is all his doing, and you must see him about it. My arrangements are all made for this winter. I cannot give you employment." Thus finding that I should not be a pleasant subject in the fort this winter [1846-47], I made up my mind to leave, bag and baggage.[1] So I immediately got some buf-

---

[1] This was the mistake of Larpenteur's life. He was a faithful, efficient, and reliable clerk of the A. F. Co., had been promoted in due course, stood well with his superiors, and was in fair way of becoming a partner of the great organization. Far better have pocketed his pique with his wages, and kept on with his employers, than turned himself adrift with nothing but a large family. He would doubtless have got even with Clark for the Fort Louis affair, if he had bided his time.

SON OF THE STAR, AUGUST, 1870.

(Died in Autumn of 1880.)

falo hides to make a bull-boat, and in two days after my arrival was under way for some lower post, hoping to be able to reach Fort Pierre. This was about the 20th of November [1846], altogether too late for such a journey; but the weather was fine and I thought I might reach some point where I could pass the winter, and thus keep out of Fort Union, where I did not think myself welcome. But the weather changed suddenly, and the next morning after leaving Union, full of ire at finding that I could not proceed any farther, I was obliged to return.

I must say that Mr. Kipp was fair enough with me. He furnished me with a room for myself and family, and provided my firewood and water, which had to be hauled from the river, all free of charge, and also allowed me to trade all the dried meat I wanted, charging myself what was thus expended. This enabled me to pass a half-pleasant winter; but, doubting that I should ever be re-engaged, I made up my mind to leave the Company, and take my family to the Flathead mission,[8] of which Father de Smet had so favor-

[8] St. Mary's Mission, which was founded in 1840, when the Jesuits first entered the Bitterroot valley under De Smet, having come overland from the east. It was held by them till 1850, when it was bought by Major John Owen, who came into the valley as a trader that year, and remodeled the mission into Fort Owen. His bill of sale for the property, dated St. Mary's Mission, Flathead Country, Nov. 5, 1850, is extant.

ably spoken to me. So I made arrangements with
Mr. Kipp to build me a boat, in which I was to leave
early enough to reach the States in time to get off
with the Mormon emigration.

According to agreement the boat was ready, and on
the 5th of April [1847] I left Fort Union with my
family, consisting of six children, accompanied also
by Mr. Latty [Latta ?], son-in-law of Mr. Laidlaw,
who had come up in the fall for his health, and two
men. We had a pleasant trip, excepting some high
winds, which sometimes caused us to remain as much
as three days camped in the willows, and one fright
from a war party of Rees.

When we stopped at Fort Clark, Mr. Des Hôtel,
who was in charge, told us that a party of 22 Rees
had gone to war on the Sioux in 11 bull-boats, two in
each boat; but remarked that there would be no danger for us, as the partisan was a young man friendly
to the whites. "This partisan is the son⁹ of Old
Star," said he, pointing to the old man, "and there
is Old Star himself"; and a very fine looking fellow he was. The following morning we left, expecting to meet them on that or the following day, as they
had started the day we arrived; but it was not till the

---

⁹ Son of the Star was the brave and wise chief of his tribe in the
'6o's–'7o's, and is believed to have died in the '8o's. He was
present in council at Fort A. Lincoln in May, 1875. The portrait
we present is said to be a good likeness.

second day, about noon, that we discovered the
party. Although we had been well armed at the fort,
and were not in much danger for ourselves, we could
not feel entirely safe, on account of my family of Assiniboines, who were deadly enemies to the Rees; for
I knew the latter to be worse than any others, in taking revenge on women. But we were soon discovered
by them, and on we had to go. As soon as we came
near they commenced to yell at a great rate, and in a
moment our boat was surrounded. All those that
could get hold grasped our boat; but this appeared to
be done in good humor. As we thus drifted along
with the current, they gave us some of their provisions,
which were little balls made of pounded parched corn,
mixed with marrow fat, and some boiled squashes;
in exchange for which we gave them some fine fat
buffalo meat. Ahead of us there was a boat which we
afterward found contained the partisan, who, having
given his orders, had gone on to find a suitable landing; and in a little while his party, who held us prisoners, landed us in his presence. He was a very fine-
looking young man, and had his pipe ready for a
smoke; but he understood so few words of Assiniboine
that I could make out little of what he said, and was
anxious to be out of the clutches of his party. I got
out what tobacco I had, a good bundle of dried buffalo
meat, and some sugar, of which I knew they were

fond, and after this made a sign that I wanted to proceed on my journey; upon which he gave me the sign
to go, charging me not to let any one at Fort Pierre
know they were under way. Under such fair
promises we took our leave of the gentlemen, having
fared much better than we expected.

On we proceeded again, quite jovial, and praising
the partisan, who we hoped might exchange his boats
for horse-flesh, as that was what the party were after,
and take some Sioux scalps, if these could be obtained. As we went along I began to think of what
kind of a reception I should have from Mr. Picotte at
Fort Pierre, which I somewhat dreaded to enter.
But as I was a free man, who owed the Company
nothing, I did not think there would be much danger
in approaching him; and if he would not let me come
into his fort, I could very well sleep outside, as I was
used to it by this time.

At last we came in sight of the fort, and as ours was
the first boat down this spring, many persons came to
the landing to see who had arrived, and to learn the
news. A little before landing, I saw Mr. Picotte at
the head of the crowd, who had made way for him to
be the first to receive us. He looked very pleasant,
and I supposed he was glad to see Mr. Latty, who
handed him the mail; but I soon found him well disposed toward us all. He shook hands with me in a

very friendly manner, and invited me up to the fort,
saying, " Never mind your baggage; I will send the
wagon for it, and for your family." This was rather
a surprise to me, who expected anything else but such
a kind reception. We walked up to the office, where
he opened the letters, read several, and after a while
said, " Larpenteur, come to my room." I could not
think what this private invitation meant, and supposed it would end in a scolding; but as he had been
so kind as to invite me into his fort, and send for my
family, I did not think it would be a very serious one.
There was no one else in his room, where he bade me
be seated, and then asked abruptly, " What made you
leave the Company?" I replied that I had not left
the Company; that I had left Clark only. After I
had related the particulars he smiled and said,
" It is true, Larpenteur, that I ought to have
written to you; yet you did wrong—you who
have been so long in the Company should have
overlooked that, knowing how much we thought
of you; and it would have been better for you,
if you did not want to serve under Mr. Clark, to
have remained at Fort Louis until the arrival of Mr.
Culbertson, who you knew was to be up in the fall."
To which I remarked that probably that would have
been better, but that it would have been very disagreeable for both of us. " Now then," he continued,

"I am told that Mr. Kipp treated you badly last winter. Did you have any words with him?" I then told him such reports were false; that I had no complaint to make against Mr. Kipp. "Well, now, here is a draft of $200 on your friend Johnson in St. Louis, in favor of the Company; what is that draft for?" "It is for provisions which I got during the winter," I replied. He then tore the draft to pieces and threw it into the fire. "Now," said he, "how much did you expect to save of your wages this year?" I told him that according to arrangements I had made with Mr. Denig, the clerk of Fort Union, I expected to save $300, if not more. "Well," said he, "come to the office; I will get the bookkeeper to make you out a draft on the Company for $300."

While the clerk was making out the draft supper was announced, and well was I prepared for that. After supper we all retired to the office, where most of the conversation was on the great discovery of gold in California, this being the first that we had heard of it; for the news had just reached Fort Pierre, and some could scarcely credit it. Mr. Picotte then said to me, "What are you going to do with your family? Are you going to settle below?" After telling him that my intention was to go on to the Flatheads, in company with the Mormon emigration, he said I should be too late for that; but, if I wished, he would give me a letter to Bordeaux, the person in charge of Fort John [10] on the Platte, where I could remain all winter and proceed on my journey early in the following spring; or, better than that, I could engage with the Company for another year, make arrangements with them to take me up as far as Fort Benton, and go from there to the Flatheads. This was very kind of him. Being prepared to go either by the Platte or by the Missouri, and convinced that I stood fair in the estimation of the Company, I left Fort Pierre next morning in great glee, holding Mr. Picotte high in my esteem.

On reaching the settlements, I learned that the Mormon emigration had gone, and that I was too late. So I went down as far as St. Joseph, Mo., where I left my family, and immediately proceeded to

[10] Fort Laramie, on the North Platte, then in charge of James Bordeaux. The great Mormon emigration of 1847 may be read conveniently in H. H. Bancroft's Works, vol. xxvi, being the Hist. of Utah, chap. x, pp. 252-274. Larpenteur was too late to join it, as it had passed Fort Laramie already, reaching the Black Hills early in June. Bancroft, p. 255, quotes an orig. MS. of 1847: " Fort John, or Laramie, was occupied by ' James Bordeaux and about eighteen French half-breeds and a few Sioux. . . . Two or three of us visited Mr. Bordeaux at the fort. We paid him $15 for the use of his ferry-boat. Mr. Bordeaux said that this was the most civil and best behaved company that had ever passed the fort.' " This year, 1847, is later than the time when it was usual to call Fort Laramie by its earlier name of Fort John: see note [11], p. 23.

St. Louis, where I arrived in time for the Company's steamer to the Yellowstone. I made arrangements to serve one season, and they were to bring up my small outfit for the Flatheads the following summer. Everything being thus arranged to my satisfaction, I took my family on board at St. Joe, and after a pleasant trip of six weeks we reached Fort Union on the 27th of June [1847].

CHAPTER XIV.

(1847-49.)

A FEW days after my return to Fort Union I was reinstated in my former department; but as some of the clerks had gone to the States, and were not to return till the fall, I had an addition to my duties, having the retail store and the men to command, besides the trade. All went on smoothly, excepting that a war party of Sioux attacked the men at the hay field, wounding one, and killing four oxen which had been hitched to the shafts of the carts, in Red River fashion. The men came running, out of breath, to report the attack, saying they thought the oxen were all killed. I then took two Spaniards, mounted the best horses in the fort, and went to see how matters stood. On our arrival at the spot, ten miles from the fort, we found three carts turned over, the animals dead in the shafts, and the fourth ox standing in a ravine with several arrows in him, mortally wounded.

The usual time for the fall express arrived, and on the 15th of October [1847] Mr. James Kipp and suite made their entrance into Union, including Mr. James Bruguière, his nephew, who had formerly charge of the retail store and command of the men. So I was relieved and had only to attend to the Indians. For some time after Iron-eyed Dog had so much troubled me, young men who called at the fort on their war-paths would ask me how I liked my comrade, the Iron-eyed Dog; to which I would very impru-dently reply that I had made my medicine for him, that I thought would be as strong as theirs if not stronger, and that they would find it out before the summer were over. Should anything happen to him after I made such a declaration my chance to escape unhurt would be small. To my great astonishment, a party of Blackfeet happened to surprise the Assini-boines during the summer and shot the Dog through the back. This was a bad shot for me, although I must confess that I was not sorry to hear of it, but the scamp was not killed. This news kept me somewhat uneasy. Harvey's Opposition boat having been ice-bound 18 miles below Union, he concluded to winter there; so a trader had to be sent from Union to op-pose him, and I was chosen, for Mr. Kipp did not like to send his own dear nephew. So, toward the last of October [1847], I was dispatched with an outfit to

build in opposition to Mr. Husband, that being the
name of the gentleman in charge. I dreaded going
to this place, for we had learned before arrival of the
Opposition that the Dog had been killed by the Rees.
At this time a good strong peace had been made with
the Assiniboines by the Gros Ventres, Mandans, and
Rees, and in the fall they would visit and trade corn.
Mr. the Iron-eyed Dog was a great gambler; he had
won a large quantity of goods from the Rees, and was
returning to his camp well packed, when a small party
of Rees overtook and shot him. My medicine was
strong! Now his brother was in the camp where I
had to go and build, on the bank of the Missouri, and
the Dog had been killed about three weeks before.
If I had been uneasy before, imagine how I felt now.

On my arrival in camp I was invited by the chiefs
and most of the leading men into their lodges, as
usual. After accepting many invitations, I returned
to my own lodge, which I found well lined with visit-
ors. A little while after I had taken my seat, hoping
that invitations were all over, a little Indian boy came
in, saying, "He invites you." Indians do not like to
mention each other's names, on which account there
is often trouble to get at the right name. At last one
said, "He is the brother of the one who was killed
by the Rees—look out for him!" "Now," said I to
myself, "here is another scrape"; but knowing the

Indian character, and understanding their language, I thought I could get out of it. So I followed the boy to the lodge. On entering, I saw a great six-footer, in full mourning—that is, daubed all over with white clay, legs full of blood, head full of mud, and hair cut short; indeed, he did look like a monster. On my entering, without shaking hands he bade me sit down, and then commenced to light the pipe without saying another word. During this time I did my best to assume a sad countenance, to correspond with his own. At last he got through with the preparation of his pipe, lighted it, and having handed it to me, said, " I suppose you have learned of the misfortune I have met with." I then answered, " Yes, we have, and on learning this sad news we were all very sorry. It is true your brother was troublesome when in liquor, but this we always overlooked, knowing it was not his fault, and, aside from liquor, he was a good man—a good robe-maker, whom the chief of the post thought a great deal of. I have heard my chief say that he thought the Dog would become the chief of the band of the One who Holds the Knife [Gauché]; and indeed I was of the same opinion." The poor fellow, or the villain, thinking by my talk that he had lost a greater brother than he had supposed, burst into a tremendous lamentation, which I did not know how to take; but it did not last long. During my confab a small wooden bowl was placed before me, filled with pounded buffalo meat and a few pieces of marrow fat; but I had already been to so many feasts that I could not partake of this. When I thought the mourning ceremony over, I told the monster my reason for not eating, said that I would take it to my family, and asked him to send his little boy with me for the pan. This is customary with them. The little boy followed me to my lodge. Having shaken hands with him, I gave the boy a large plug of tobacco, put some hawk-bells, some vermilion, a knife, and various small trinkets in his pan, and sent him back. My success was so great that I got all this man's trade during the winter,[1] and he remained my best friend. So much for having buttered him so well!

During this winter [1847-48], myself and James Bruguière, who each had an Indian family, formed a partnership to open trade with the Flatheads. We sent down our requisition and were to go up in the

[1] While Larpenteur was at this outpost he was visited by Palliser, from whom we hear of him by name: "Next morning [in March, 1848] . . . we rose early and reached Mr. Larpenter's [*sic*] post late in the evening. This was a very miserable hut, and the supply of dry meat with which he and his companions were provided was so small, that I made but one day's halt," Palliser, 1853, p. 191. Palliser reached Fort Berthold a few days later, on Apr. 1, 1848.

keel boat to Benton, where we were to proceed to the
Flatheads with a wagon and pack-horses.   Mr. Culbertson had moved Fort Louis down the previous
spring [of 1847], this being the season after Fort
Benton was built.[2]

[2] We thus discover the close date of abandoning Fort Louis,
after establishment of Fort Benton in 1846.   For the latter, see
L. and C., ed. of 1893, p. 355.   Benton fell heir to all the glories
of Union when the latter succumbed to Buford; it became an em-
porium, the entrepot of the whole northwest.   In the winter of
1862–63 about 35 persons lived at Benton.   In 1864 it was sold by
the A. F. Co. to the N. W. Co.; in October of 1869 it was occupied by U. S. troops, mainly as an entrepot for Fort Shaw, on
Sun river, and Fort Ellis, on the Gallatin near Bozeman, both of
which posts started in 1867.   Before 1865, the steamboat arrivals
had ranged from none to 4 each summer; there were 8 in 1865,
and next year the number leaped up to 31.   This was exceeded
in 1867, when 39 arrived; there were 35 in 1868, and 42 in 1869.
Those were four great years for Benton—1866–69.   Immediately
after military occupation the arrivals fell off to 8 in 1870, 6 in
1871, 12 in 1872, 7 in 1873, 6 in 1874, etc.   This last was the year in
which I made Benton my point of departure in a small open boat,
on a voyage of 835 miles down the Missouri to Bismarck.   The
town which grew up about the post had a boom about 1882–83,
when no fewer than 27 steamboats reached Benton one summer.
When the St. Paul, Minneapolis, and Manitoba branch of the
Great Northern Railway was brought past, it killed the river
trade, and the importance of Benton began to wane in favor of
Great Falls, which latter it was the policy of James J. Hill and
Paris Gibson to build up.   When I again stood on the spot, Oct.
15, 1893, I viewed the crumbling ruins of disused Fort Benton,
close to the river bank, about the lower end of the town,
which reached a mile or so up river.   Relics of departed great-

The steamer, which never failed, arrived on time [in the summer of 1848], bringing up our requisition. Being put in charge of the keel boat I started on my second trip to the Blackfeet. Unfortunately for us the river was even lower this season than it was last and we were 90 days on our trip. The Flatheads had news that we were coming, and as they were at peace with the Blackfeet, a party had come to Fort Benton, thinking it was about time we arrived. They had been disappointed, but left word where we could find them, saying they would assist us over the mountains; but we were frustrated in this good thing.

A band of Blackfeet, called the Little Robes,[3] after

ness still stood at the water's edge, in the shape of snubbing-posts at which the boats used to tie up; but the shriek of the locomotive told another story as the train rattled by the bluffs, a mile and a half back of town. Charles Rowe, who was keeping a shack called the Overland Hotel in 1874, was in 1893 mayor of the town, besides being proprietor of the Grand Union Hotel, two squares from which were still to be seen the ruins of Fort Campbell, so named for Tom Campbell, a great character in those parts when I was there in 1874. The ford was still used when the river permitted, but an iron bridge spanned the Missouri.

[3] These do not appear to have been a well-known band. De Smet, Oreg. Miss., etc., 1847, p. 326, has the following: "The Black-Feet nation consists of about 14,000 souls, divided into six tribes, to wit: the *Pegans*, the *Surcees*, the *Blood Indians*, the *Gros-Ventres* (descendants of the Rapahos), the Black-Feet (proper), and the *Little Robes*. These last were almost entirely destroyed in 1845." Catlin also speaks of the Little Robes as a band of about 250 lodges, early in the '30's. De Smet's Gros-

the name of their chief, instead of following the rest
of the tribe north after trade was over, remained on
the south side of the Missouri. Some of Little
Robe's young men happened to have a fight with the
Flatheads; some one of each party was killed and
horses were stolen. So the peace was broken, and
the Flatheads returned to their country as fast as
they could. This was bad news for us, as the peace
had been an inducement for us to undertake this
trade.

Still, go we must, and horses must be had, which
could not be procured without going to Little Robe's
camp to trade them; and there was some risk in that.
At this time Mr. Clark was in charge of Benton, and
I must say he did all he could for me. He lent me
horses to go to the camp and also sent his interpreter
with me; a very good one he was, and had he not been
with me, it is doubtful whether I should have returned. The second day after we left the fort we
came to the camp; it was yet early, and the horse
trade soon commenced. This was going on finely,
when an old rascal commenced a harangue, in which
he said, " Why do you trade horses to that stranger?

Ventres are not those so called on the Missouri, otherwise the
Minnitarees or Hidatsas, but the Grosventres of the Plains or
Prairies, otherwise Fall Indians or Atsinas, an Algonquian tribe
confederated with the Siksikas or Blackfeet proper: see Henry
and Thompson Journs., 1897, pp. 530, 531.

He wants them to take arms to trade with your enemies. You had better take what he has, and send
him home," and a great deal of other bad talk, which
at last induced them to take back their horses, for
which, however, they returned to us very nearly the
correct payment. All this was owing to my interpreter, for, had any other than him been with me,
they never would have brought back anything, and
most likely would have taken our pile. At last he
said, " We had better pack up and leave; the longer
we stay the worse it will be for us." Taking his ad-
vice, we packed up and went away, leaving the old
scoundrel still at his harangue, and having been able
to retain but two horses out of eight which we had
traded. After this bad luck, we reached Fort Benton
next day.

As the season was far advanced, we had no time to
wait for the return of the Indians from the north, nor
did we think it advisable to do so under the present
circumstances. Through the kind efforts of Mr.
Clark, we were furnished with two wagons, two carts,
and eight pack-horses, besides the four horses to each
wagon, and two to each cart; also, with ten men, and
a good guide—at least, one who was thought good.
It was about the end of October [1848] when we
left Fort Benton again. As our horses were not well
broken to harness, we had some trouble for the first

few days, after which we went along about half right. On the fourth day out we reached Sun river [4] early. My hunter had been in luck, having killed three grizzly bears, and he brought to camp the meat of the cubs, which, at this season, are very fat. It was but fun for this hunter to kill them. He came into the mountains at the same time I did, with Robert Campbell [in 1833], and had remained all this time in and about them; he had been hunter for Captain Stewart, who came out from England two seasons in succession to hunt in the Rocky mountains.

While the fat cubs were boiling we dug the bank of Sun river to make a crossing place, mine being the first spade ever sunk in this ground by a white man, and my wagon the first to cross this stream, in the year 1848. After a good dinner we hitched up again; the river was fordable, with a good gravelly bottom, and our crossing was made without much trouble.

[4] Medicine river of Lewis and Clark, falling into the Missouri from the W. immediately above the series of falls on the latter, at the town of Great Falls: see L. and C., ed. of 1893, pp. 371, 373. It is 63 m. from Fort Benton by the trail to Fort Shaw; most likely the point at which Larpenteur struck Sun river was near this fort, at the crossing now called Sun River. Shaw was first started as Camp Reynolds, June 30, 1867, when Major Wm. Clinton of the 13th Infantry, with four companies, selected the site, 20 m. up the river; but on Aug. 1 of that year the name was changed in honor of Col. Robert G. Shaw, 54th Mass. Vols., killed at Fort Wagner July 18, 1863.

We camped a short distance below the ford, where
we had plenty of grass and wood. Our guide, who
was a young Piegan Indian, had not been seen since
breakfast, as he knew we were acquainted with this
part of the country. We thought he might have
gone in search of deer or bighorns, and were not uneasy about him till it became dark, when some began
to think he had deserted us; at bedtime he had not
made his appearance, and in the morning we found
ourselves without a guide. Now what to do was the
question. No one knew the way to the Flatheads,
even by a foot path. I thought of my hunter, who
was accustomed to travel through mountains, and
proposed to take him with me, and try to find the
Flatheads.

The next morning we started, thinking we had
given our guide sufficient time to make his appearance. Expecting to find game, we took nothing with
us but a little sugar and coffee; but we were mistaken
in that, for when one gets in the mountains he is out
of the range of game, as I found out afterward.[5] On
the fourth day, when on the summit of a mountain,
there was a heavy snow, and we had eaten but one
partridge and two ducks since the day after we left
camp. After this fall of snow, having found no prac-

[5] Larpenteur does not tell us where he struck the mountains,
but if he had known where to find Lewis and Clark's Pass, he

ticable wagon road, nor even any fit one for pack
animals, we concluded to turn back.

At this time we had already been three days without
eating. Now the fine dreams of well-set tables commenced, with no conversation at noon or at night

would have had little difficulty in taking his wagons over into
the Bitterroot valley, and no trouble whatever with his pack animals. In the fall of 1893 I drove in a spring wagon nearly to the
summit of the pass, surmounting the last few hundred yards on
foot, in the traces of wheels which had gone over. An account
of this trip, with details of topography, appeared in the Inde-
pendent of Helena, Mont., Oct. 17, 1893, and probably other
Western newspapers. The road goes up Green creek, a tribu-
tary of the middle fork of Dearborn river, and the pass lies
between the two heads of Green creek, which I named North
Pass creek and South Pass creek. I found some other branches
of Green creek which are as yet unmapped, one of which I called
Burch's, after Mr. J. H. Burch, one of my companions. I left the
railroad at Cascade, on the Missouri, and easily made the round
trip in 2¼ days. See L. and C., ed. 1893, p. 1077, *et seq.*

That is a beautiful piece of country to travel in—that area
inclosed by the Missouri on the E., the Continental Divide on
the W., Sun river on the N., Dearborn on the S. It is broken
enough to be full of first-rate landmarks, and open enough to
show them all off—everything as plain as the squares on a chess-
board. When I started from Cascade to climb the main chain of
the Rockies I had nothing to go upon but a mental image of
Lewis and Clark's Pass, on top of which I proposed to stand.
The natives of what had long been Lewis and Clark Co. could
tell me nothing of any pass of that name; the snowy summits of
the range before me revealed nothing but inaccessibility. I had
been assured there was but one way over the main Divide,
namely, Cadotte's Pass, which I knew all about and cared noth-

Enlarged copy of a portion of
Lewis & Clark County Montana,
showing
Green Creek, Lewis & Clark Pass & Cadotte Pass.
also
Capt. Lewis return trail as placed
thereon by Dr Elliott Coues.

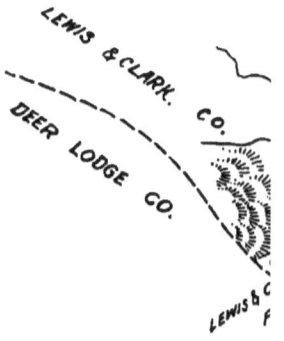

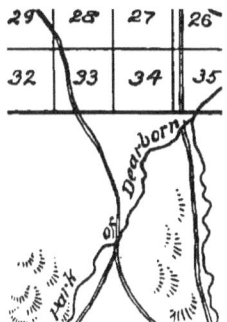

camp, and this lasted three days longer. On the morning of the sixth day of our starvation my hunter found a mare and colt. Having traveled about two hours, we perceived a party of warriors; but, fortu-

ing about. But I heard from one person of another pass, called Pend d'Oreille, said to be somewhere N. of Cadotte's ; and was satisfied that this was the one I wished to reach when I learned that an old Indian trail from Sun river led to this Pend d'Oreille gap—for, did not Captain Lewis follow an Indian trail from his pass to that river, July 7, 1806? Then I found a young fellow named Michael Casey, who said he knew nothing of any pass, but could put me on that old trail. Enough—we started. The first thing I recognized was Shishequaw mountain of L. and C., which stands out so strongly as Heart mountain on Stevens' bird's-eye lithograph, but which Casey called Haystack butte. Having followed up the N. fork of Dearborn river far enough, through a curious place I called the Gates of Dearborn, we approached the foot of the great range at a point marked by twin hills, which the people who live under them have named Sunrise buttes. Next morning, not long after the sun had gilded their tops, I was on the trail, retracing Captain Lewis' footsteps ; and the sun at his meridian scintillated through a whirl of sparkling snow blown off surrounding mountain tops as I stood breathless on the crest of the Great Divide, in the tracks of the original explorer. A few days afterward the Surveyor General of Montana, Mr. George O. Eaton, in whom I discovered a gentleman who had assisted me to embalm the body of an officer killed by a stroke of lightning near Fort D. A. Russell, Wyo., in 1877, was kind enough to reduce my rough topographical notes to scale, and give me a blue print ; from which has been made the map now facing the reader. I believe it to be the most accurate delineation we possess of the approach to the pass by the Indian trail which Captain Lewis followed down from the Divide en route to Sun river.

nately for us, we saw them first, turned back a few
steps, and then struck for the roughest part of the
mountains to hide and select a good place for defense,
in case we should be found.   During this rambling
I thought of a dried buffalo sinew which I had in my
bullet pouch to mend moccasins.   I pulled it out and
cut it in two, offering my hunter a part of it, which
he refused, saying, " Eat it all; I believe I can starve
better than you."   So, without asking him a second
time, I soon demolished the sinew, which I found excellent, except that it was too small.   We at last
found a good hiding place among the rocks, where
we remained concealed till near sunset, scared and
mighty hungry.   The mare was a fine, fat one,
but she had gone lame in one of her hips.   My
hunter, being by this time perhaps as hungry as I
was, went out of our hiding place, and very soon I
heard a shot.   He came back, saying, " We shall have
plenty to eat now."   " What have you killed? " I
asked.   " I have shot the old mare," he replied.   We
both got a piece of the liver and some ribs, went to
a place where there was wood, near by, made a small
fire, and began to cook.   The liver we threw on the
embers, but the coals of tamarack pine turned it so
very black that, at first, I thought it impossible to eat
any.   On digging pretty well into it. I found some of
it eatable; but this was laid aside when the fine fat ribs

were roasted. The fat tasted excellent, but the lean part was rather insipid, and appeared to need a great deal of seasoning to make it palatable. As bad luck would have it, we had forgotten our salt at last night's camp; so I tried sugar, but that was worse than without.[6] However, we made a fine supper, and grew a little more talkative. In the morning, having looked around as well as we could, to see if we could discover Indians, and found no signs of any, we made up our minds to get under way again, and did so, taking with us a good supply of mare meat. We now traveled without fear of starvation, though our great uneasiness regarding enemies rendered the journey very unpleasant; but we were so fortunate as to reach camp the next day, having seen nothing alarming. We found them all right in camp, but without much to eat, meat being all out. I offered them some of the meat I had, but when they found out what kind it was they declined, saying they thought they could hold out a while longer. As I did not have much left, and had got used to it by this time, I was not sorry for their refusal, now that I had pepper and salt. I can assure the reader that horse meat makes excellent steaks.

[6] This locution, which I leave as I find it in Larpenteur's MS., reminds me of the little boy who, being asked to define salt, replied, "Salt is what makes soup taste bad if you don't put it in."

Finding no road, winter advancing, fear of war parties—all those things taken into consideration induced us to make up our minds to turn back and winter at Benton. This move, which was the best I could make under the circumstances, was anything but consoling to me. I knew that I was a ruined man. Aside from the danger apprehended on our return to Benton, my situation was an awful one; but there was no alternative. Next morning we got under way for Benton. On the following day, in the afternoon, we discovered Indians on the other side of the Missouri, yelling with all their might and making signs for us to come to them. This gave us a great fright, the women and children crying and going on at a great rate, knowing that we could not reach timber in time should the enemy rush on us. Yet nothing better could be done than to try to make the timber. Had it not been for the women and children, we would have stood our ground behind our wagons, but on their account we made for timber. In the meantime we saw the Indians going up the Missouri, not appearing to want to cross; and, applying the whip pretty sharply, we finally reached the so-much-desired timber, where, losing no time, we forted the best we could, expecting an immediate attack. Night came without further alarm, and arrangements were made for a good strong guard. Just after we had retired a tremendous croaking and cawing of crows was heard, which brought all hands up again, much frightened. The women and children being as well secreted as we could, every man stood to his gun, awaiting the attack; but, when an hour or more passed and nothing happened the fright subsided, and all came out of their hiding places—I mean the women folks and children. Then the talk was that it was a bad omen to hear crows croak at night, and my Canadians had a long sitting up, relating their superstitious stories. I thought that the crows might have been frightened by Indians, who, seeing us thus put on our guard, had concluded to delay the attack until morning. So the same guard was continued, and after a little all was quiet again.

Morning came and all was right. My hunter, who had got up earlier than the others and gone to see what he could discover, soon returned, saying that he had found out why the crows made such a noise last night. The party of Indians we had seen had passed through the timber, where they had killed two elk, taken most of the meat, and gone on their way. The crows had feasted on part of it, when Mr. Bruin, coming for his share at night, had frightened the birds away from their repast. This was the whole cause of their alarming noise. Luckily for us there was more meat than the bear and all the crows could eat, and my hunter brought enough of their leavings to make us a good breakfast. We were soon hitched up and ready to start, hoping to reach Benton the next day, provided we met with no accident on the way. Our hopes being realized, we entered Benton, all safe and sound.

Upon arrival we were informed that the Indians we had seen were those who had killed the elk we had found. They were a party going to war on the Flatheads, and had left the fort shortly after we did, having been told that we were on our way to the Flatheads, and warned not to trouble us if they saw us. They were Piegans—good Indians, who promised not to harm us; and we afterward learned from a couple of them that they had seen us and made signs for us to come after meat; but, seeing that we were frightened, kept on their way.

At the time we returned to Benton, the Indians had commenced to arrive from the north. Among them was a small Indian named Sata,[1] a half-breed Flat-

[1] De Smet,Oreg. Missions, etc., 1847, p. 328, speaks of this Indian by name, in amusingly theological terms. The good father is on his way from St. Mary's Mission in the Bitterroot valley, and is approaching Fort Louis on the Missouri, Sept. 22, 1846, when he thus vouches for his proselyte, neophyte, acolyte, or whatever the mongrel ex-pagan may have been: " SATA, our interpreter, acts the part of an Apostle—after each interpretation, he resumes his discourse, and speaking from the abundance of his heart, produces a powerful effect upon his audience. The word *Sata*

head and Blackfoot, who had guided Father De
Smet and others from the Flathead mission.   He
said he could find a wagon road, and if I wished would
show me the way.   Having been inspired with con-
fidence in him by the people of the fort, and being
anxious to see the Flatheads, wagon road or no
wagon road, I determined to try that famous guide.

does not differ in signification from *Satan*, and as the Indian
generally receives his name from the natural disposition he man-
ifests, we may safely conclude, when such a name is given to a
Black-Foot, that the grace of God has operated most powerfully
in converting this savage to what he is at present." With which
pious conclusion we might agree, if we could imagine this ety-
mology of the name *Sata* to be as sound as we have no doubt
De Smet's theology would be found by anyone who could understand such comical twaddle.

In October of 1893 I traversed the entire valley of the Bitterroot from Missoula to the summit of Gibbon's Pass, up one side of
the river and down on the other, on the double trail of Lewis and
Clark, in an ambulance furnished at the instance of the Secretary
of War by my old friend, Col. Andrew Sheridan Burt, commanding
Fort Missoula. On the 25th I passed through Corvallis, where are
still visible the ruins of Fort Stevens, built in 1853 by Lt. John
Mullan, and named in honor of Gov. Isaac I. Stevens, for whom
was also named Stevensville, Ravalli Co., Mont., where I slept that
night. On the S. W. flank of Stevensville is St. Mary's Mission,
a small church built of chinked hewn logs, with a dwelling in the
rear and some other buildings, the whole shaded with large cot-
tonwoods, planted on three sides of a square. On the W. is a
graveyard, in the middle of which stands the monument of Father
Ravalli, a fellow-worker with De Smet, beloved and respected by
all for his good deeds. The lot is about 20 x 20 feet, inclosed
with metal rails and chains on low marble posts; in the center rises

The third day after my return to Benton I was on the way again, taking one of my men who understood the Blackfoot language well. I was mounted on a fine stuball[8] horse, much fancied by Indians, well dressed and well equipped; my man was also well arranged, and we felt sure this time of seeing the Flatheads. The first evening, about camping time, we fell in with a small camp of Blackfeet, who invited us

the monument, about 14 feet high, consisting of a granite pedestal with a marble plinth and square tapering shaft surmounted by a cross marked I. H. S. in German text. The inscription is : '' Montana's Tribute to Father Antony Ravalli S. J. Who spent forty years in this far west, for the good of souls and suffering mankind, as a zealous missionary and charitable physician. Died Oct. 2, 1884. R. I. P."

[8] *Sic*—for *skewbald*, meaning spotted askew or irregularly with white; equivalent to *piebald*. *Skewbald* is a fair word, which will be found in most dictionaries, though now obsolescent or provincial. But it may not be generally known that *skewball* or *stuball* survives in the West, or did survive till the Civil War at least, when either of these words formed the refrain of some nonsense-verses that made an immensely popular, uproarious drinking-song. I first heard it at Fort Larned on the Arkansaw in 1864, when I was a slender, pale-faced, lantern-jawed, girlish-looking youth, without a hair on lip or chin and hardly dry behind the ears—what would I not give to look like that now? Anathema Maranatha, Tempus edax rerum! I do not recall the song intact, but it largely consisted of '' When Johnny comes marching home again, *skewball!* says I " ; and " We'll all drink stone blind, Johnny fill up the bowl ! " How often it was dinged into my startled ears on the particular occasion to which I refer may be inferred from Pike, ed. 1895, p. 426.

to stay over night with them, and we willingly did so, saving ourselves the trouble of making camp.   But it was not long before I repented of having accepted the invitation.   I soon felt a crawling in my under-clothes, and by morning it seemed as though I were being raised clear out of bed.   I before never felt so miserable in my life, and in spite of all I could do, I could not get rid of the lice till I returned to Benton.

Our next encampment was at the Great Falls of the Missouri.   The noise was so great that we could scarcely hear each other talk, but I could very well feel the graybacks hunting for their suppers in my shirt.   Sata happened to kill a fine buck and we had a glorious supper.   Having traveled for two days without any unusual occurrence, pretty much on the same kind of road as on my former trip, we reached the base of the mountains.   Sata remarked that we had best try to get some meat, as game was scarce in the mountains, and now was the time to provide for ourselves.   Thinking myself somewhat of a hunter I went a little ahead of the party next morn-ing, and soon saw some objects crossing a small brook, at so great a distance that I was unable to dis-tinguish whether they were men or game.   Hoping they were deer, I slipped the cover off my double-barrel, and went after them.   When in the act of shooting, I discovered on my left, behind a small hill, an object which I could not make out, but thought was probably a wolf. Sata and my man, who had come up by this time, asked me, " What have you seen? " I replied in Blackfoot, " Matahpey," meaning " people." On our advancing a few steps, fifteen naked Indians, with guns, bows, and arrows rose up before us, ready to shoot; but Sata cried out, " My brothers! my brothers! don't shoot! It is I." Hearing this they put down their arms, came up, and shook hands. They said, then, that they had discovered us, taken us for beaver trappers, and had made arrangements to kill us. As to myself, whom they took to be the chief, they had me killed already in imagination; one was to have my stuball horse, one my sky-blue coat, another my gun, and so on in the partition of my effects. The object I had taken to be a wolf was one of the Indians, who remarked himself that he had got a little nearer me than the balance of his party, and that I might be glad his gun was hard on the trigger; for he had aimed well at my breast, and I surely would have been a dead man, had he got his gun to go off. On learning where we were going, they told my guide that it was impossible for us to cross the mountains; that they had had great trouble to return, and that our animals could not get over. Thereupon, my Sata gave up the idea of going any farther, and concluded to turn back with them.

So there was another trip for nothing, except gathering an awful crop of graybacks, which I thought would devour me before my return to Benton. The Indians were delighted to see us turn back, immediately struck out on a hunt, and at the place agreed upon to encamp, came in with three fine deer, of which little was left in the morning. This was a party of young men, full of fun and mirth. I could not have been better treated than I was by them. On arriving in camp my place was prepared for me; the best spot was made as soft as it could be, by pulling and cutting small willows on which to spread my bedding. Then the best pieces of meat were cooked in various ways, and given to me first of all. There were roast and boiled meat, liver and guts broiled on the coals, blood pudding—in fact, all that was considered eatable of the animals. They kept this cooking going on almost all night—it is incredible what a quantity an Indian can eat. With the exception of such feasts nothing took place on our return worth mentioning, and on the fourth day after falling in with this party we entered Fort Benton again.

Although all my efforts had been in vain, I did not yet abandon the idea of the undertaking, which I intended to put through early in the spring. Eight or ten days after my return, I was taken with a pain

in the breast, which I laid to my starvation and exposure, and the failure of my undertaking. I could
not help taking my disappointment to heart, and this,
I believe, was the cause of a great derangement of my
nervous system, from which I never completely recovered. Mr. Culbertson, who had returned from the
States, treated me extremely well, and I passed as
pleasant a winter [of 1848--49] as could be expected,
situated as we were.

During this winter the whole tribe of the Blackfeet learned that our intentions were to proceed to
the Flatheads in the spring, and remonstrated
against it. The leading chiefs advised us not to go,
saying that it would not be good for us, even if we
succeeded in getting there safe; that we would not be
safe when we got there; that there would be war
parties constantly about the Missouri; and that the
tribe would not go north as usual, but would remain
south of the Missouri, with the intention of carrying
on war with the Flatheads.

This information, from such sources, induced us to
abandon the project. We sold out to the Company,
and early in the spring [of 1849] went down to Fort
Union with Mr. Culbertson. We left Benton in a
large Mackinaw boat. Having started so early, we
were sometimes ice-bound, and suffered a great deal
from cold. The water was very low, and frequently

we had to jump into the river to get the boat off sand bars, while there was ice running. I was generally one of the first in and last out of the water. Twenty days out from Benton we landed at Union.

On my arrival I was offered $1000 a year to take charge of Fort Alexander, which, at that time, was considered the most dangerous post the Company had. But, wishing to take my family to some place where I could open a small farm, on which they could remain, should I return to the Indian country, and feeling sick besides, I refused the offer.

While at Union I learned that the Company wanted to sell Vermilion post. So I concluded to go down and see what I could do in that line. I procured a small canoe, hired one man, and started for the States. There I was, again on the march, in a hollow log, for the distance of 1200 or 1500 miles. Luckily, this time I reached Trading Point[9] without any accident,

[9] In Iowa, Mills Co., on or near boundary of Pottawatomie Co., about the 653-mile point of the Missouri, nearly opposite Bellevue, Sarpy Co., Neb. The first thing ever named here was Camp White Catfish of Lewis and Clark, given as 10 m. N. 15° W. above the mouth of the Platte, where the explorers rested July 22–26, 1804 : L. and C., ed. 1893, pp. 52, 54. The name of Trading or Traders' Point seems to have lapsed : but the vicinity was noted during many years for the sites of various establishments which have left their traces in such names as old St. Mary's, Sarpy's, Bledsoe's, etc. Bellevue appears as the only permanent one of them. This was once a trading post of the Mo. F. Co., of

and remained there awaiting the arrival of the Company's steamer to return to Union. On my way down I stopped a few days at the Vermilion post, but was not pleased with it, and abandoned the idea of making any arrangements there.

At last the steamer arrived. I went on board, where a letter was handed to me from my father, saying that he had sold his farm near Baltimore, and gone to St. Paul with my brother Eugene, to assist him to settle there, and also to see his grandson, A. L. Larpenteur.[10] He was then to proceed to France, which he wanted to see once more before his death, and then to return and die in America with his children. He urged me strongly to leave the Indian country and settle near the rest of the family, where what property I might have, with what he could do for me, would enable me to live more comfortably than I could while wandering in the Indian country, exposing myself to the risk of losing my scalp.

which a Mr. Dougherty was in charge in 1833; on the dissolution of this company it was bought by Mr. Fontenelle, who sold it to the Government when he was appointed Indian agent, and settled a few hundred yards lower down. St. Mary's bend was cut off in 1879, and the latest chart I have gives the landing for Bellevue as 11.3 m. above the mouth of the Platte.

[10] Owner of the original MSS. upon which the present work is based. Address The Anchorage, 341 Dale St., St. Paul, Minn.

Situated as I was, this news was well calculated to revive my hopes; but being born for bad luck, my agreeable expectations were not of long duration. Yet I had some pleasant moments, thinking that I should meet my old father again, whom I had not seen since 1838, and be united again with all the family after a separation of upward of 20 years; and I began to think that perhaps it was well for me not to have reached the Flatheads.

On reaching the Vermilion I was informed that a gentleman had just arrived from St. Paul, across the country, to take the census of the Santee half-breeds; and, at the same moment, the person himself came on board. After being introduced I asked him if he was acquainted with A. L. Larpenteur, to which he replied, " I know him very well." I then asked him if he knew whether that Mr. Larpenteur's grandfather had come from Baltimore. He answered in the affirmative, but added that he had bad news for me; which was that the old gentleman had died the third day after arrival at St. Paul, and that he, my inform-ant, had attended the funeral.

I will leave the reader to imagine my feelings, and to sympathize with me, if there is any sympathy in him. The steamer is pushing off, and I must re-sume my journey, as well as my story.

During my short stay at the Vermilion, on my way

down, Mr. Culbertson had overtaken me there, also
on his way to meet the steamer; but, learning that
there was cholera on board, he made up his mind to
go no further, and to return to Fort Pierre.   His reason for going to meet the boat was that they apprehended difficulty with the Indians at Crow Creek [11]

[11] " Crow creek " is a name of no fewer than three streams
not very far apart, above White river and below the Great Bend
of the Missouri.   The term refers to the bird, not to Crow Indians; and the nomenclature has led to so much confusion that
the following explanation may be serviceable:

1. The name Crow creek originated in *Corvus* creek of Lewis
and Clark: see ed. of 1893, p. 118.   This stream falls into the
right (W.) bank of the Missouri at the 1064-mile point of the
Mo. R. Comm. charts, about 8 m. above the mouth of White
river.   Lewis and Clark passed it Sept. 16, 1804, and camped a
mile above.   This stream became the American river of Nicollet's map, and the American Crow creek of Warren's and later
maps.   A place at its mouth was called Oacama, and here was
established the Brulé Agency.   Five miles higher up, at the
1069-mile point, on the other side of the Missouri, is Chamberlain, seat of Brulé Co., S. Dak., on a small stream now called
American creek, by duplication of part of the name of American
Crow creek, but formerly Rantesha river of Nicollet, and Cedar
Island river of Warren.   This higher creek falls in opposite that
Cedar island which is the Second Cedar island of Nicollet and of
Warren, and which was the site of old Fort Recovery.   Nicollet marks " Old Ft. Aux Cedres " directly opposite this island,
on the W. (right) side of the Missouri, but perhaps its position
was the same as that of old Fort Recovery.   Maximilian, Trav.,
p. 147 of the ed. of 1843, says: " . . . the 25th of May [1833], we
had already reached the White river, and at noon came to a
place where the Cedar Fort, a trading post of the Missouri Fur

Agency, in case their annuities were not on board.
So Mr. Culbertson told me, privately, of his writing
to Mr. Sarpy, who was in charge, to tell him, in case
the annuities were not on board, to send a dispatch to
Fort Pierre, and he would come down and help to
pass the boat; but, if they had the annuities, it would
not be necessary for him to be there. At this time

Company, had formerly stood. When the Company was dis-
solved, this and other settlements were abandoned, and demolished by the Indians."

2. Ascending the Missouri about 12 m. from Chamberlain, or
to about the 1081-mile point, we come to a place where, on a
ridge of bluffs, an Arikara village once stood and was destroyed
by the Sioux; opposite which was Fort Lookout, a post of the
French Fur Company. "Sioux Agency, or, as it is now [1833]
usually called, Fort Lookout, is a square, of about 60 paces, surrounded by pickets. . . Close to the fort, in a northerly direction, the Fur Company of Mr. Sublette had a dwelling house,
with a store; and, in the opposite direction, was a similar post of
the American Fur Company," Maxim., p. 148.

3. We are now nearing the celebrated Trois Rivières des Sioux,
the Three Sioux rivers, or Three Rivers of the Sioux Pass of L.
and C., ed. 1893, p. 122. These fall into the left bank of the Missouri not far apart—the first two of them about a mile apart, say
at 1082 and 1083, with a bluff between them ; the third one
about 2 m. higher up than the second. Opposite and below
their mouths is the very large and shifty island called Prospect
or Laurel (French Isle des Lauriers). Directly opposite the two
first of the Sioux rivers, on the right (W.) bank of the Missouri,
at the 1082½-mile point, was Fort Hale, whence the road led to
Red Cloud Agency. Now, as to the names of these Three Sioux
rivers: The *first* or lowest one of them became Crow creek, and
I know no other name for it. The *second* became Wolf creek,

Major Hatting, their " father," [12] a young man of about 26 or 27, was on board.

Five or six days after we left the Vermilion post we arrived at Crow Creek, or as it was called, the Collins Campbell houses. After the boat landed, three barrels of hard-tack were put ashore, with some sugar and coffee, and given to the Indian soldiers; after which the men were sent to take in wood, which was all ready for the boat. In the meantime the Indians, who had not been invited on board, as was customary, took offense, and knocked the heads out of the barrels of hard-tack, which they threw into the river;

also called Pokende by Nicollet, Shompapi by Warren, and Elm by Heap. The *third* became Campbell's creek, also called Chanpepenan by Nicollet and Caswell by Heap. On this third one of the Sioux rivers was Campbell's old trading post. This stood some little way up Campbell's creek, opposite the 1085-mile point of the Missouri, on the W. bank of the creek.

4. Higher still, at the 1089-mile point, a *fourth* creek comes into the same side of the Missouri as the Three Sioux rivers ; and its name is *Crow* creek again, duplicating the name of the First Sioux river. It is the Sniyan Otka creek of Nicollet, and has also been called Soldiers' creek. On this was Fort Thompson, and the Crow Creek Agency. This *place*, as distinguished from the stream itself, became known as Crow Creek; and Crow Creek became also the name of the large Indian reservation which extended from about the position of old Fort Lookout, far up the Missouri, to above the Great Bend, and included portions of several counties of South Dakota.

[12] Indian agent. In another place Larpenteur is very severe in his remarks on Major Hatting: see last chapter, beyond.

then they horsewhipped the men away from the
woodpile, and placed a guard at the line; after
which the chiefs, without invitation, came on board.
After they had seated themselves one got up and said,
" It is customary, when the boat arrives, to invite us
on board, to shake hands, and tell us the news.
What is the matter with you this year? Do you think
that we have got the itch? Is that the reason you
don't wish to shake hands? " Being told that their
father was on board, they asked if their annuities
were also on the boat. On being answered in the
affirmative, they said, " Do you intend to take them
to Fort Pierre? " Having been told that was the intention, the Indians remonstrated, saying they had
been promised that the annuities were to be distributed at this place, and that they would have them
left here; for they had nothing to do with the fort.
The agent, giving no decided answer in this regard,
went and sat down near the chiefs, who were all holding their heads in expectation of some reply from their
father. Things were thus at a standstill for some
time; but at last a tall, robust Indian got up, saying,
" I am not a chief; but I am a soldier. I see that my
chiefs all hang their heads down, as though they did
not know what to say or do. But I know what to
do." With that he struck a heavy blow with his tomahawk on the table, and then, addressing himself to the

agent, said, " Hold up your head—when you speak with chiefs or soldiers, look them in the face. You are young, but we suppose you must have some sense, or our great father would not have sent you up here. My chiefs have spoken, but it seems that they have not been heard. I am a soldier; I tell you that those goods were promised us here, and they will not go any farther. I know that all the chiefs are not here yet; but we have sent for them. If you think that we want to distribute the goods during their absence you can put them in the store, and keep the key until they come; but we will not go to the fort. Do you hear that? That is what I have to say as a soldier."

The Indians were perfectly correct. I was on board the boat last season, when Major Matlock,[13] at this very place, made them the promise and made up their requisition for the goods now on board; the Indians were then well pleased, and the major said he would throw in a box of sugar as the tail, which was 500 pounds.

During this great debate a cup of coffee and a hard tack had been presented to all who were in attendance, and as soon as the soldier and speaker was

[13] This Indian agent also fares badly at Larpenteur's hands, as will be seen in another part of his work, where he passes in review the numerous agents with whom he was personally acquainted.

through, they all took leave. Upon consultation
among the authorities it was agreed to unload the
annuities—a very prudent forced move; and the following morning we were permitted to depart. Those
Indians had been much displeased, the year before,
with the behavior of the agent; they had shot at him
while on board, but missed him, and killed one of the
hands instead. We reached Union early in July
[1849].

CHAPTER XV.

(1849-55.)

WITH the intention to proceed to St. Paul I got all my family on board, and shipped for St. Louis, and thence for St. Paul. On examining affairs it was found that my father had not had time to accomplish his will properly. I went to Baltimore, applied to the Orphan Court, and had the will broken. All being arranged to my satisfaction I was ready to return. Being still sick, I applied to a physician, Dr. John Buckly, who said that a sea voyage might prove beneficial to me. So I embarked on a small merchant ship, and in 45 days landed in New Orleans. I put up at the St. Charles Hotel, where I remained a week; but the climate did not appear to agree with me, and I took a steamer for St. Louis.

About the latter end of February [1850] I arrived in St. Louis, where I had to remain until navigation opened to St. Paul. During my stay I made arrangements with the Company to take charge of the Vermilion post,[1] on condition that, if I chose, I could purchase it at a certain stipulated price. About the 15th of March I left for St. Paul. When the boat reached Galena it was learned that the ice on Lake

[1] At date of May 16, 1843, Audubon's Journ. i, 1897, p. 493, has: "Then we came to the establishment called that of Vermilion River, and met Mr. Cerré, usually called Pascal, the agent of the Company at this post, a handsome French gentleman, of good manners. He dined with us. After this we landed, and walked to the fort, if the place may be so called, for we found it only a square, strongly picketed, without portholes. It stands on the immediate bank of the river, opposite a long and narrow island, and is backed by a vast prairie, all of which was inundated during the spring freshet." This is present Vermilion Prairie, on the borders of Union and Clay counties, S. Dak., and part of Buffalo Prairie of Lewis and Clark, Aug. 23, 1804 (see ed. of 1893, p. 83), or Hutan Kutey Prairie of Nicollet, extending up to Vermilion river. The post was some miles below the river, for Audubon goes on, passes some bluffs on his left hand, and stops "about ten miles below the mouth of the Vermilion river." Again, on Oct. 27, returning down the Missouri, Audubon passed Vermilion river at 7.30 a. m., and did not reach Fort Vermilion till noon. Next day he left the post at 8 a. m., and "landed 15 miles below on Elk Point." The Missouri has undergone such great vicissitudes hereabouts, especially by the immense cut-off of 1881 at present Vermilion, S. Dak., that it may be impossible to say now how many channel-miles below the mouth of the Vermilion this Fort Vermilion was situated ; but its position was in S. Dak., at a point of Vermilion Prairie nearly on the line between Union and Clay counties, on the Kate Sweeny bend, opposite Ionia, Neb., at the 849-mile point, now some 10 m. by river below the town of Vermilion, and some 45 m. by river above Sioux City.

That this was the site of one Vermilion post I am assured ; that this was the post of which Larpenteur took charge in 1850 is

Pepin was still too strong, and we had to remain a few days longer. At last the captain concluded to start. On arriving at the lake, it was impossible to get through, and as it appeared to the captain that

probable, but questionable. I am credibly informed of a post known as Fort Vermilion much higher up the Missouri, above Vermilion river, about halfway between the latter and " Jim " river—say 10 m. from each by the trail. This position would be at or near Audubon point, about the 876-mile point of the Missouri by Mo. R. Comm. charts, directly opposite the mouth of Petit Arc or Little Bow creek of Lewis and Clark, Aug. 26, 1804 (Hopa Wazupi river of Nicollet, present Bow creek), in Clay Co., S. Dak., about 2 m. S. S. E. of the point where the boundary between that and Yankton Co. strikes the Missouri. A Vermilion post was built at this place in or before 1835, in which year Wm. Dixon or Dickson was in charge, and afterward Théophile Bruguière. The latter is a person of whom Larpenteur speaks beyond ; his wife is living, and she and another pioneer, named Joseph Leonnais or Lyonnais, now of Sioux City, who were both at a Fort Vermilion in 1836–37, insist stoutly that the post they knew by that name was the one in question *above* Vermilion river, halfway up to the James. A third pioneer, named Letillier, also of Sioux City and also interviewed on the subject in my behalf by a friend, attests that a certain Fort Vermilion was above Vermilion river " when Théophile Bruguière was in charge."

Evidently two different establishments, about 25 m. apart, are in question ; and Larpenteur himself fails to inform us where *his* Vermilion post was situated. It was *not* the Ponka post of which he was afterward in charge, on the Niobrara. One Le Clerc had a small fort at the mouth of this river, on its right bank, opposite old Fort Mitchell ; but I never heard of any post called Vermilion in that vicinity.

we would be likely to be detained there long, he pre-
ferred to return to Galena. After waiting there a
week we again started. The ice was still strong, but
by main force, cutting the slushy ice like an old ram,
the boat succeeded in getting through. I believe it
was on the 8th of April that she landed at St. Paul,
being the second boat up that season.

I remained in St. Paul until a St. Louis boat arrived,
which was on the 15th of April. Next day I got all
my family on board for St. Louis. On my arrival
there, the Company's steamer was not yet ready to
start; so I took my family up to St. Charles to await
her arrival. On the 10th of May the steamer arrived,
and I went on board, bound for the Vermilion post.

About a week after we got under way cholera broke
out among the men below, and grew so bad that we
boxed up three and four at a night. The boat at last
stopped. We put everything out, aired and limed the
boat well, and about eight days afterward started
again. The disease abated, though there were a few
more cases, among which was my woman; but she
recovered. Finally we reached the Vermilion post,
where I was deposited for one year, very glad to get
out of that steamer.

The post, the country, all pleased me well enough,
but I found there was nothing more to be made in
the Indian trade, and the place was too much ex-

posed to hostile Indians for me to remain there as a farmer. The Indians robbed me of all my corn, as well as all the half-breeds who were settled near the post; they were obliged to abandon their places and most of them went to settle at Sergeant's Bluffs.[2] Had my health been good, I should have enjoyed myself well that winter [1850-51].[3] Trade was not bad, and there were good hunting grounds. One young Indian went out turkey hunting by moonlight, and returned in the morning with 14 fine large turkeys.

[2] In Woodbury Co., Ia., on the Sioux City and Pacific R. R., 6 m. by rail below Sioux City, and 2 m. from the left bank of the Missouri. The village borrowed its name from that of the bluff at Sioux City on which Sergeant Charles Floyd of Lewis and Clark's expedition was buried, first on Aug. 20, 1804, next on May 28, 1857, and for the third time on Aug. 20, 1895. See Report of the Floyd Memorial Association prepared on behalf of the Committee on Publication by Elliott Coues, Sioux City, Dec., 1897, 8vo, pp. 58. There is every prospect that the purpose of the Association will soon be realized, in which event a towering shaft, visible for many miles up and down the river, will replace the lowly "seeder post" which originally marked the lonely grave of the first U. S. soldier known to have been buried west of the Mississippi.

[3] The date is confirmed by a letter of Father Christian Hoeken, dated Post Vermilion, Dec. 11, 1850, to De Smet, pub. in the English ed. of the latter's Western Missions and Missionaries, New York, 1859, p. 266: "Mr. Charles Larpenteur, whose hospitality you have often enjoyed when travelling in the desert to visit the Indian tribes, is now in charge of the post, and he received us with all the goodness of a father," etc.

I traded six of him, among which one weighed 24 pounds.

Finding that the Vermilion post would not suit me, and learning that there were good claims to be had cheap down about Little Sioux [4] river, I sent my clerk to see how it looked there, and if possible to purchase for me a certain claim which, from the description given, I thought would be likely to suit me. The situation was about 85 miles [5] from this place

[4] Petite Rivière des Sioux of the early French traders; Eane-ahwadepon of Lewis and Clark, who passed its mouth Aug. 8, 1804; Inyan Yankey of Nicollet's map; Sioux Pictout river of some writers. This stream falls into the left bank of the Missouri, from the E., in Harrison Co., Ia., at the 722 mile of latest Commission charts, about 88½ m. below Great Sioux river. The railroad crosses near its mouth, at a place called River Sioux, a mile below another named Little Sioux, both on the S. (left) bank of the stream. " The sources of the Little Sioux river are in Minnesota. The Ocheydan branch issues from the West Okabena lake in Township 102, Range 40. The eastern fork, bearing the name Little Sioux, rises in the West Heron lake in Township 102, Range 37. These lakes are on the divide between the Mississippi and the Missouri rivers and have an elevation of 1580 feet above the sea. The Little Sioux river has a total fall, from its source to its confluence with the Missouri in Township 81, Range 45, of 500 feet. Measured upon the axis of its valley it has a direct length of 150 miles. It has been meandered for a distance of 98.7 miles from its mouth with a direct distance of 42 miles—a proportion of 2.35 to 1." (Legend of Vincent's Map of the Western part of Monona Co., l: 79,200, Sept., 1896.)

[5] By river Little Sioux is 84½ m. below the railroad bridge at Sioux City, and this is 54½ m. below Vermilion, S. Dak. Total,

[Fort Vermilion]. On his return he said that
the claim was a good one, but that it had not
been represented correctly; for, in order to have
it right, I must purchase a part of the neighboring claim, and that being the case, I had better
go and see for myself. A few days afterward I
went down, made the purchase to suit me, also arranged to have a ferryboat built, and then returned
to my post. At the time I am speaking of there was
no settlement between Sergeant's Bluffs and the
place I bought—a distance of 50 miles.⁶

About the 15th of May [1851], when Mr.
Honoré Picotte came down from Fort Pierre in a
Mackinaw, I embarked with him, bound for Sergeant's Bluffs, from which place I intended to go
down to my claim by land. We had had a great deal
of rain; the Missouri, as well as all other streams,
had overflowed their banks, and the bottoms were all
inundated. I had to remain about 15 days at Sergeant's Bluffs, waiting for the roads to become practi-

139¼ m. by the channel of the Missouri. But the distance by land
is of course much less. As traveled by the road from Sioux City
to Little Sioux it is 55 m., to which add about 25 m. for Larpenteur's journey from Fort Vermilion down to Sioux City, or a
total of about 80 m. by land.

⁶ From Sergeant's Bluff to his place on Little Sioux river Larpenteur had a journey of just about 50 m. to make by the road.
Almost all of it was in the flood-plain of the Missouri, with

cable.   I purchased four Indian ponies, two French carts, and hired a guide, at $2 a day, to pilot me through the water, for there was very little dry land to be seen between this and my place.   About the last of May or first of June, my guide said he thought he could get me through; so we hitched up and started. The fourth day, after traveling through mud and water, we reached a place called Silver Lake.[7]   Our

which that of the Little Sioux coincides for a long distance. Hence we can understand the great inundation which he proceeds to describe.

[7] Silver lake is a small, slender body of water, about a mile long, connected with a large horseshoe-shaped slough which was once the bed of the Missouri, as was the similar adjacent Blue lake.   The latter is the Coupée à Jacques through which Lewis and Clark navigated the Missouri, camping on it Aug. 9, 1804, and again Sept. 5, 1806: see ed. of 1893 at those dates, p. 71 and p. 1204.   Silver lake lies for ¼ of its length in section 2 of Lincoln township, Monona Co., Ia., adjoining the village of Whiting, on the Sioux City and Pacific R. R., and has been artificially connected with Skunk lake.

Larpenteur is traveling approximately along the present line of the Sioux City and Pacific R. R.   The reader who would like to see what an inundation Little Sioux river can sometimes make, should look at my friend Mitchell Vincent's blue print of the overflow of 1892, when 143,000 acres were submerged—47,000 in Woodbury Co., 88,000 in Monona Co., and 8,000 in Harrison Co. The flood reached Onawa, where Mr. Vincent resides, but fell a little short of the railroad, except for a few miles near the mouth of the Little Sioux.   The waters through which Larpenteur struggled in 1851 appear to have been still deeper and more widespread.

ponies were then nearly broken down, although they had not made over 35 miles during the four days. As this was the best part of the road, my guide said that it would be impossible for us to reach my place with the carts; that we still had 25 miles to make; " and," said he, " you have not seen anything yet; wait till we get near the ferry." He advised making horse travailles, which consist of two long poles, tied about three feet apart and extending eight or ten feet at the far ends, which drag on the ground, with cross-bars fastened to them behind the horse, so as to make a kind of platform on which plunder is loaded.

The travailles being thus prepared, and the children loaded on them, we proceeded on our journey. Having made about 10 miles, we camped at Laidlaw's[8] grove, which was afterward called Ashton's grove, and goes by that name still. We were then 16 miles from my place, which we had to reach next day or camp in the water, as there was no dry place to be found. We could have made that distance easily in

[8] Ashton's grove occupied sect. 32 of present Ashton township, Monona Co.; town laid out by Isaac Ashton in 1854; seat of the county till 1858, when its existence ended by removal to Onawa. The place is a mile or so N. of Onawa, close to the railroad, on the W. of the latter; present Ashton ditch runs through it, parallel with Silver lake ditch—both these ditches being connected with Card lake, another old cut-off from the Missouri. Larpenteur's reckoning of 16 m. to his place on the Little Sioux is about right.

a half day had the road been good.   We rose early, and having placed the children to the best advantage on this kind of conveyance, got under march, not expecting to stop to lunch, as there was no fit place. On we went, my guide taking the lead; I behind him, leading a pony, and my woman behind me, also leading one.   The nearer we came to the ferry, the deeper the water became, and the sun was already approaching the western horizon.   Finally it came up to the armpit of my guide, and the children were dragged almost afloat on their travailles, crying and lamenting, saying, " Father, we will drown—we are going to die in this water—turn back."   At times the ponies were swimming, but there was no use of turning back; the timber on dry land ahead was the nearest point; there was nothing to be seen behind us but a sheet of water, and the sun was nearly down. So on we pushed—on, in spite of the distressing cries of the children, whom we landed safely on dry ground just at dark.

We had not eaten a bite since morning; but the children were so tired, and had been so frightened, that they laid down, and, in spite of the mosquitoes, which were tremendously bad, went to sleep without asking for supper.   This was certainly one of the most distressing days I had ever experienced; but we old folks felt like taking a good cup of coffee after such a day's work. A fire was immediately made, the coffee was soon served, and no time was lost in turning in for the night.   Next morning we did not rise very early, but took our time, got up a good breakfast, and then called out for the boatman.   Mr. Condit and Mr. Chase,[9] the gentlemen of whom I had purchased the place, came to ferry us over, and in a little while I was in my log cabin, about 15 feet square.   As I had left the carts and my effects at Silver Lake, I left the ponies on the other side, intending to return next day; but as it seemed impossible to bring my stuff through that deep water with my ponies and carts, I arranged with Mr. Chase to meet me with a yoke of cattle hitched to a large canoe. With that understanding, I started next morning with my guide; we pushed the march, and reached Silver Lake about ten at night.   Then a tremendous dark cloud rose in the west, and just as we were going to take supper—about the hour of eleven—it blew a hurricane, or, rather, a whirlwind [cyclone], which took our lodge clear up in the air, and then blew the fire into the baggage.   It was all we could do to save our plunder, and the lodge we did not find

[9] Silas Condit and Amos Chase, both Mormons, associates in the first settlement at the mouth of the Little Sioux. Mr. Vincent informs me that Mr. Chase was an enterprising, upright man, who died about 1887.

till next day. The latter was so suddenly taken up
that we felt like two fools for a moment, not knowing what had become of it. Our supper, as you may
say, was good as gone; but, fortunately for us, it
was all wind. When we got up in the morning we
found that a great many things were missing from
our baggage, and much time was lost in searching
for lost articles which had been blown so far off by the
hurricane. Having succeeded in finding them, and
made ready for a start, we saw a wagon coming from
above with four yoke of cattle, and I found it was my
old friend, Théophile Bruguière, an old Indian trader,
and the first settler at the mouth of Big Sioux river
[Sioux City, Ia.]. On his approach he cried out,
" Hello, Larpenteur! what in the devil are you doing
here? You're in a pretty fix, aint you? " " Yes,"
said I, " and I'm mighty glad to see you." " You
are, hay? Well, put some of your stuff in my wagon
—bet you I see you through." Bruguière was one
of those plain, good-hearted sort of men, who would
help anyone out of such a scrape. Having thus arranged matters, we got under way, and camped that
night at Laidlaw's grove. Early next morning we
again got under way, and, being so well fixed, had
little difficulty in reaching the ferry. I must not omit
to say that we met Mr. Chase, who had been as good
as his word, about four miles this side of the ferry,

coming to meet me with his oxen and canoe; but we did not need his assistance, and left him to follow us empty.   We reached the ferry in time to cross, and, all this trouble being over, I was soon safe in my [10]

[10] Larpenteur nowhere tells us exactly the location of his cabin, but I am fortunately able to supply the required information through Mr. Vincent. It was in Harrison Co., Ia., 2¼ m. S. of the boundary of Monona Co., in the N. E. ¼-sect. of sect. 18, tp. 81 N., range 44 W. 5th princ. merid., about 2 m. N. N. E. of the town of Little Sioux, and 3¼ m. in an air line N. E. of the mouth of Little Sioux river, near the left bank of this river, opposite Cochran's bridge. In a letter to me dated Onawa, Dec. 22, 1897, Mr. Vincent writes: "In the fall of 1851 Larpenteur built a tavern and established a ferry at the point said. It was a log structure, surrounded with a number of out-buildings and trellises; everything was whitewashed that would hold lime, and according to descriptions which old settlers have given me the collection of buildings presented a picturesque appearance. I have lately visited Fontainebleau, as Larpenteur called his place, in memory of that near which he had been born in France, and found his widow, now nearly 80 years of age—a fine-looking, black-eyed old lady, who must have been a beautiful girl. She is a native of Vermont, and very intelligent, though now of the defective memory of old age. I also visited Larpenteur's grave, in a ravine near the site of his old home. It is under a low, spreading, red cedar, marked by a small marble tombstone on which is the inscription ' Charles Larpenteur. Died Nov. 15, 1872. Aged 69 years, 6 months, 7 days.' He kept a journal until his death. After finishing the entry for any one day it was his custom to set down the date of the day following. He last wrote the date Nov. 15, 1872, and to this a neighbor added ' Charles Larpenteur died to-day.' This explains the local tradition that Larpenteur ' wrote the day of his death.' "

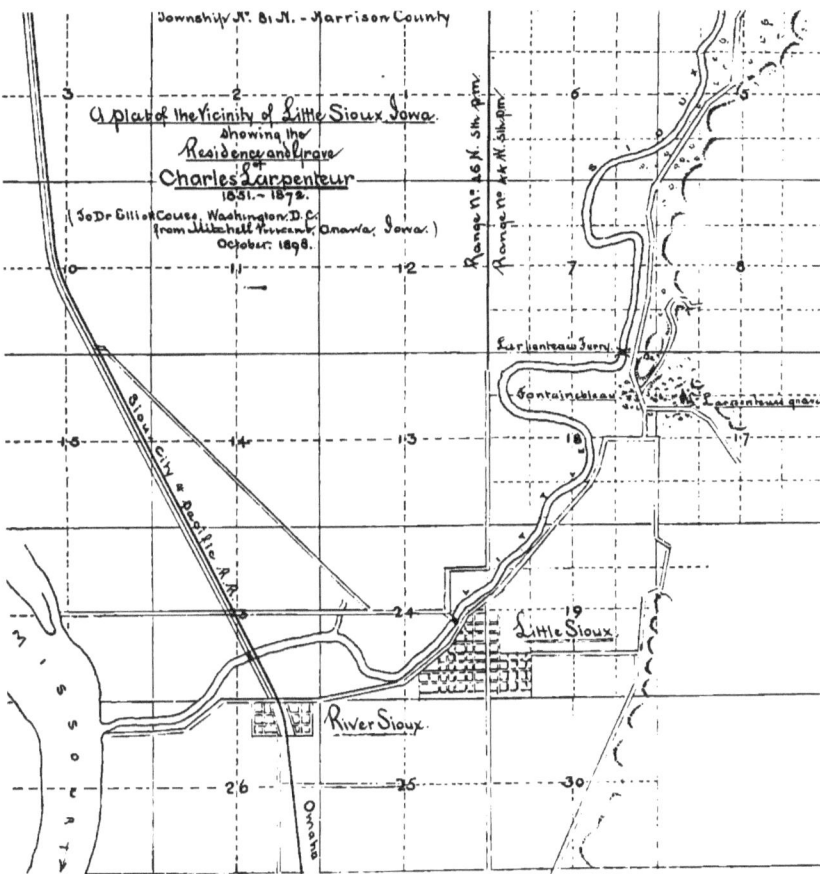

cabin. We had as good a supper as our means could afford, and after much talk over the eight days out from Sergeant's Bluffs we retired for the night.

Although there were a few Mormons scattered in this part of the country, it might still be considered an Indian country. It was occupied, at the time, by Omahas, and frequent parties of Sioux went back and forth to war on the Omahas and Ottos. After I had arranged with Mr. Amos Chase to get me out logs for a house, and provided for my family, I started for St. Louis to raise what funds I had in the Company's hands, and also to procure some groceries. On my return I found most of my family down with the ague. Mr. Chase had gotten all the logs out, and I immediately began to build, but, as there were no mills, I had to hire a sawyer to work with a pit saw.

About November [1851] I got into my house. But a short time afterward a small party of Omahas came to trade, who had the smallpox, unknown to me. In a couple of weeks my smallest child, a beautiful little boy, took the disease and died the third day. His mother fretted so that she never fairly got over it.

During the winter I made arrangements with Mr. Peter H. Sarpy to go up to Running Water, to take charge of his trading post for the Poncas. In the spring [of 1852] I rented my place, left my family on it, and early in April started for the Niobrara, or Running Water. The post, a very poor establishment, was situated immediately on the bank of that river, about a quarter of a mile from the Missouri.[11]   I had but three laboring men, and one cook. That summer I had no other pastime but that of fishing, and had to smoke away mosquitoes every evening.

In September [1852] the news came that all my children had died. I did not think this possible— some might have died, but not all. Not long afterward I received a letter from Mr. Sarpy, saying that I

[11] There have been several trading posts at and near the mouth of the Niobrara, Rapid river, Running Water, or L'Eau qui Court of the French—the latter a term often rendered Quicurre and in several similar forms : see L. and C., ed. 1893, p. 107. The best known was Fort Mitchell, situated immediately at the mouth of the stream, on the bluff point of the left bank. One Le Clerc, an irregular trader who had done well enough in the A. F. Co. to set up for himself, built a small post just above, on the other side, in 1840 or earlier; this had been abandoned May 21, 1843, when Audubon passed, as he says, Journ., p. 504 : " We stopped to wood at a very propitious place, for it was no less than the fort put up some years ago by Monsieur Le Clerc. Finding no one at the spot, we set to work cutting the pickets off his fortifications till we were loaded with the very best of dry wood." We presently learn from Larpenteur the date of disestablishment of Sarpy's post, when he ceases to have it in charge. There is now the new town of Niobrara in the extensive bottom land on the lower side, snug under the bluff; and a pile bridge spans the stream a mile and a half from its mouth. Ponka creek falls into the Missouri the same distance above the mouth of the Niobrara. The position of the latter is 131 m. by the channel of the Missouri above the Big Sioux, in lat. 42° 46' N., long. 98° 03' W.

had lost two of my children.   No end to bad luck for me!

The Poncas were a small tribe, who made but few robes.   Having been accustomed to large tribes of Indians, and to big trades, I did not pay much attention to them, and have nothing to relate except one little incident which happened in the early part of the winter [of 1852-53].   After Indians have gone on their usual hunt, more or fewer loafers always remain about a post, instead of following the main camp, and become a great nuisance.   Just such a set remained here—about six lodges in all.   There were six able-bodied men among them; we were but five, all told, and as the laboring men had to be out, only myself and the cook remained at the post.   The Indians became such beggars that I was obliged to refuse them a great many things; and they appeared so regularly at meal times that I became disgusted, and sometimes told the cook not to give them one mouthful to eat.   One morning they came into my room, after my men had gone to their work.   They took their seat on the floor, and I could perceive that there was some dissatisfaction in the assembly.   I called to the cook to come in.   This cook was a Frenchman from St. Louis, named Louis Ménard, about six feet three, weighing about 130 pounds; but though he had no belly he looked as though he might swallow the big-

gest Indian of the lot.   He was an old voyageur, who
had been with Frémont on his trip to California.[12]
Just after he came in an old Indian, who had not appeared with the first ones, entered and bolted the
door inside.   I observed this, but said nothing.
Several of those Poncas could speak Sioux, and one
of them got up to make a speech, which, of course,
was to find fault with my way of treating them.
By the discourse I began to see that they intended to
take advantage of there being none but us two in
to force me to give them eatables.   I had a small
squaw ax under my bed, which I took out and handed
to Louis.   I then drew my pistol from under my pillow and placed my gun near at hand.   Surprised to
see these maneuvers, without saying another word
they immediately rose and left the room, somewhat
faster than they had entered it.   This put an end to
their begging and loafing, and I afterward gave them
a cup of coffee only when I thought proper.   Some
days after this incident they came and made an
apology, requesting me not to say anything about
it to the chief when he returned from the hunt.

The Poncas, at that time, were divided into two

[11] The name of Louis Ménard appears in the lists of engagés
of both of Frémont's expeditions—that to the Rocky mountains
in 1842, and that to Oregon and California in 1843–44: Rep., 1845,
p. 9 and p. 105.

bands, one led by a chief called the Whip, who kept on this side of the Running Water, and the other named the Drum, who remained on Ponca creek. Those two chiefs were jealous of each other, and it was thought that they would become hostile.

This winter's trade was small, and we were now so close to settlements that it did not pay to keep up the post; so it was abandoned. I was thus the last person in charge of the Vermilion, and at the Ponca. I had great sport hunting deer at this place. The Indians being out on their winter hunt, I remained the only hunter at this place. We had a great deal of snow, which brought the deer into the wooded points along the river, where they were so plentiful that I killed five in one day with small shot.

Early in the spring [1853] I returned to my farm. The individual to whom I had rented it died in the summer; but he had done well, and I had 40 acres well broken and fenced. During my absence the travel had greatly increased, and settlers were now coming in fast, so I rented my farm and devoted my attention entirely to the traveling community. Notwithstanding the increase of the settlements, the Omahas continued to hunt in their old grounds, and I always kept a few trinkets for their trade. All went on quite smoothly through the summer—good crops, plenty of travel.

About midwinter a party of Sioux, who had gone
to war on the Omahas, killed four of them, and stolen
some ponies, passed my place on their return. The
day they arrived being extremely cold, they concluded
to camp on the river bank near my house. While
camped there some of the young men went out hunting, and killed a deer in the timber below my field.
They brought in a part of it, and one of them told
my woman where he had hung the balance in a tree,
a short distance from the house, saying that they did
not want it, and if she chose to go after it, she was
welcome to do so. Early next morning the party
left; toward noon the weather moderated, and she remarked that she had a mind to go after that meat. I
told her to do as she pleased about it, and she finally
concluded to go. Wrapping up warm in her blanket,
and taking her daughter along, she started in quest of
the meat. As I was building a bridge at the time, I
was left alone at home, my men being all out getting
out timber. She had been gone but a little while
when a party of six Omahas came in. From their
daubed appearance I soon found out that they were
in pursuit of the Sioux, and became alarmed about
my woman; for, although they knew her well, and
were aware that she was an Assiniboine, and therefore belonged among the deadly enemies of the Sioux,
yet they looked upon her as a Sioux, as she spoke

that language. I did the best I could to induce them
to stay long enough to give my woman time to return, but they appeared in a great hurry, and soon
started. Just as they were stepping off the entry I
saw her coming home, about 300 yards from the
house. When she saw them approaching she exclaimed to her daughter, " My daughter, we are
lost! " She knew who they were, knew their customs,
and rightly judged that her time had come. On
meeting her they shook hands; but the next thing
was the report of a gun, and she fell dead, shot
through the heart. One among them then wanted
to shoot her daughter, but he was not permitted to
do so, being told, " We have killed her mother—that
is sufficient." This deed was done as quick as lightning; then, throwing away some of their little effects,
they ran off as fast as their legs would carry them.
The alarm was given, but to no purpose. My wife
never said a word, having been instantly killed. She
was also struck across the face with some kind of
blunt weapon. Her daughter was about 18 years of
age. One year afterward I married again.[18]

[18] April 12, 1855, is the date. The lady was the widow of
Lucius Bingham, who died at Little Sioux, Harrison Co., Ia., in
July, 1852 ; she had been Miss Rebecca White, of Chester Co.
Vt., b. May 3, 1818. She was the second Mrs. Bingham, became
the third Mrs. Larpenteur, and is still living, in her 80th year, as
we have seen, note [18], p. 298.

CHAPTER XVI.

(1855-61.)

FORT STEWART AND THE POPLAR RIVER POST.

ALL this time[1] the travel increased fast, and as I built considerable, I found myself a little in debt in the crisis of 1857. Seeing no show of getting out of debt without making too great sacrifices, I concluded to engage to the firm of Clark, Primeau, and Co., to go and take charge of Fort Stewart, 35 miles above Fort Union. This fort was built during the time of the firm of Frost, Todd, and Co., who, having been too extravagant, were obliged to give it up.[2]

[1] "All this time" should cover the years 1855-58, as we have kept Larpenteur's chronology straight to his marriage in 1855; and now, after a few words regarding 1857, we resume his adventures in 1859—a date written "eighteen fifty nine" in his own hand.

[2] Fort Stewart was established in 1854, and its site can be given with absolute precision, as one of the chimneys is still standing—or was very recently. This relic may now be, or could lately have been, seen ⅜ m. S. of the G. N. Ry., 3¼ m. W. of Blair sta., about 4¼ m. E. of Calais sta., and 1 m. N. of the Missouri at the point where the river now rounds into Devil's Bend. The position is in an open plain thus far from the river,

306

On the 7th of June, 1859, I took passage at Sioux
City on Captain Throckmorton's steamer, whose
name I have forgotten. On the 24th of the same
month I was landed at my post, and again among the
Assiniboines. I found this fort in a very bad condition, but in the course of the summer I got it in
order, and had very comfortable quarters. I had not
seen the Assiniboines during the last six years, and
believe I was about as glad to meet them again as
they were to see me. As I was now working for the
Opposition, against the " big house," I had to use
all my knowledge and experience to draw them to my
side. In order to effect this I had to dress some of

but was once immediately upon the edge of a former bend, which
reached fully up to where the railroad now passes. I find by
plotting the courses and distances given by Lewis and Clark for
their voyage on Apr. 30, 1805, that they went around such a great
bend as I indicate, well up under the bluffs on the N. side; but
the river now washes the opposite bluff, on the S., 2¼ m. away.
All this is made land, in the flood-plain, and now extensively
wooded along both banks, with the open ground between the
woods and the railroad. The geodetic position of the chimney
is lat. 48° 08' N. very nearly, long. 104° 43' W. very nearly. More
broadly speaking, the site is in Dawson Co., Mont., in the S. E.
corner of the Fort Peck Indian Reservation, 4¼ m. directly W.
by S. of the mouth of Big Muddy creek, and about 57 channel-
miles of the Missouri above the mouth of the Yellowstone. I
passed the place June 25, 1874, and again Nov. 8, 1893; on the
former occasion I made it 38 m. by the wagon road from Fort
Buford, and Larpenteur's 35 m. from Fort Union is near enough:
ee L. and C., ed. 1893, pp. 289, 290.

the big chiefs, and make presents to some of the leading men.   On the first arrival of any Assiniboine I
would make inquiries about such a one, and about
that other one, whom I had known, saying that I had
made up my mind to make these individuals some
little presents.   I knew this would flatter them, and
at the same time, they must have the presents they
expected or my inquiries would not have the desired effect.   So they would come to me, in the best
of humor, and, after some conversation, would say,
" Is that so?   I understood you have made inquiries
about me."   And I could observe that every Indian
was delighted to find that I had asked after him.   I
proceeded in this way through the whole tribe, and
soon had them bound to give me almost all their
trade.

   This [1859-60] was the pleasantest winter I ever
spent with the Assiniboines.   We had great dances
and talks, which always ended with a treat of a large
kettle of mush sweetened with molasses.   Although
my name was White Man Bear, in their language
Mato Washejoe,[3] the buffalo dance was my favorite,
and we also sometimes danced the bear dance.   What
had brought me very high in their estimation was
that, buffalo being very plentiful, during summer and

---

[3] From *mato*, bear, and *washichu*, white man.   This was a frequent complimentary title or soubriquet.

winter they made surrounds, in which they killed plenty of meat within 300 yards of the fort. My trade this winter was very good, consisting of 300 robes, beside a great many other skins; but the firm, fearing the American Fur Company, consolidated,[4] and as they needed but few clerks or traders, I was thrown out of employment. I was not very well pleased with Mr. Clark, who had promised to take care that I should have a good place. Those gentlemen, seeing that they had the country to themselves, reduced the number of their clerks, and the wages also; they even cut down on their men and Indians.

On my way down the Missouri I found, at Fort Berthold, Jefferson Smith,[5] an old trader, who, like the

[4] This statement is corroborated by Boller, who also enables us to check Larpenteur's date of 1860. At p. 20 of his Among the Indians, he says : " The American Fur Company (Upper Missouri Outfit) had their sway for many years. During most of the time they had more or less opposition, principally from traders who had been at sometime or other in their employ. These traders were generally well sustained by the Indians, who fully appreciated the advantages to be gained from competition. In 1860 this competing interest was bought out by the American Fur Company, with the expectation of monopolizing the entire trade of the Missouri, as in early days. In 1866 they retired from the field they had so long occupied, under which such striking changes were going on."

[5] This worthy is pictured in Boller in the following terms, p. 205 : "A hunting party was soon made up, headed by Jeff Smith, a veteran of over thirty years experience. He wore a

balance, was out of employment, and who had about
$4000.   There I also met a young man by the name
of Boller, who said that he could raise $2000 from his
father in Philadelphia.   I felt sure that I could obtain my share from Mr. Robert Campbell in St. Louis.
Under such an understanding we agreed to meet in
St. Louis.   My plan for taking up our outfit was to
go around by the way of St. Paul, thence on to Pembina, and through part of the British possessions, with

close fitting, white blanket skullcap, coming low down over the
forehead, beneath which peered the deep-set gray eyes and sharp
countenance of the old 'Kee-re-pe-tee-ah,' or Big-Bull, as the
Gros Ventres called him.   A well-worn blanket capote, once
white, but by exposure to the weather and the smoke of the
lodges turned to a sickly yellow, with leggings and moccasins
of elk-skin, completed his dress.   An excellent rifle, in a plain
skin cover, lay across the pommel of his saddle, and the han-
dle of a long butcher-knife projected beyond the parfleche
scabbard in his belt."

Jefferson Smith was living at Fort Berthold in 1866, when Boller
came by, and is again mentioned, p. 416 : " During the short
time we remained here I had the pleasure of greeting many of
my former acquaintances.   Pierre Garreau, Malnouri, and old
Jeff Smith were still living where they had passed so many
years."   Dr. Matthews, who knew him well, tells me that Smith's
descendants still (1898) live on the Berthold reservation, and that
Malnouri's first name was Charles.   He is no doubt the person
who has given name to Maneury Bend of the Missouri, as I find
it spelled on my charts, which also mark the site of a Fort
Maneury there.   This place was in the bend said, about 25 m.
above the Little Missouri and 153 m. below the Yellowstone by
water.   Mr. Malnouri is still or was lately living at Berthold.

the view to avoid the Sioux. This was a road which
no one of us had traveled. As those men had to
wait for the return of Mr. Chouteau, who had gone
up to Fort Benton, it was not till the last of July
[1860] that we met in St. Louis. I had arrived a few
days before, and had informed Mr. Campbell of our
project, of which he approved, and readily advanced
me my portion of the outfit. I also informed Mr.
Kenneth McKenzie, who knew something of that
country; he said that my plan was a good one, and
wished me success, adding that he was sure I would
do well. One of Mr. Campbell's clerks by the name
of Robert Lemon joined the company. A few days
after the arrival of the other two partners we went
into operation, Mr. Boller having obtained by tele-
graph the amount required. Our opposition move
was soon reported to Mr. Chouteau, who said that it
would prove an abortion; that we would never reach
our intended points. I was to go to the Assiniboines,
at the same place as last winter [1859-60]. Smith
and Boller were to winter at Berthold. Our equip-
ments were soon ready and shipped to St. Paul,
where we were to purchase our cattle.

On the 5th of September [1860] we left St. Paul
with eight wagons and eleven men. Our train, at
this early time, attracted the attention of many as we
went along; we were often asked where we were

bound, and on telling our destination, the answer
would be, " Why! you are going a roundabout way
to the Yellowstone! You will not get there this
winter." We could have taken Governor Stevens'[6]
route, which would have been somewhat shorter, but
this would have taken us among the Sioux, whom I
wanted to avoid, as well as all other Indians, hostile
or friendly, as I knew such meetings were always ex-
pensive and bothersome. We had some little trouble
at the start, as our cattle were not well broken; but it
did not last long. The weather being fine, we traveled well. We crossed the Red River of the North

[6] Isaac Ingalls Stevens, whose well-known Report of Explorations of 1853-55 occupies vol. xii. of the Pacific Railroad Reports,
pub. 1860. General Stevens was an officer of the regular army,
who graduated from West Point at the head of his class in July,
1839, served with distinction in the Mexican war, and resigned
March 16, 1853. Having conducted with signal ability the survey just indicated, he became Governor of Washington Territory. At the breaking out of our Civil War he became Colonel
of the 79th N. Y. Infantry, rose to be Major General the following year, and was killed at the battle of Chantilly, Va., Sept. 1,
1862. I well remember him when he was living on 12th Street
near E, in this city, just before the war; his son Hazzard Stevens
was with him—a young fellow about my own age. He and my
father were great friends ; my father's astronomical work entitled
Studies of the Earth, 4to, Washington, D. C., 1860, was dedicated
to "Honorable Isaac I. Stevens, of Washington Territory, as a
tribute of respect for his talents and high attainments in science;
and in acknowledgment of his generous friendship."

at Georgetown,[1] and thence struck for Pembina. This part of the road was quite level, well watered, and sufficiently wooded. About the middle of October [1860] we reached Pembina. There we crossed on a very poor bridge near the mouth of Pembina river. Next day we proceeded 30 miles up this river to a small village called St. Joseph, at the base of Pembina mountain, inhabited by Canadian French half-breeds. Many of my acquaintances who had been on the Missouri had settled at this place, where I almost felt myself at home and had no trouble in procuring such a guide as I wanted. I told him that I wished to avoid all Indians, if possible—my friends, the Assiniboines, as well as all others; and to find a good practicable route for my wagons, even if it took us out of the most direct road. Upon which he replied that he could take me exactly as I required, and that he knew all the camps we had to make from the start, for he had the map in his head. Being asked what his charge would be, he said that he should want two buffalo horses, meaning runners which can overtake buffalo. This price agreed upon, we left next day.

[1] A village of Clay Co., Minn., opposite Trysil, Cass Co , N. Dak., on Red river at the mouth of Buffalo river, 15 m. N. of Moorhead : see my Henry and Thompson Journs., 1897, p. 147. The reader who may be interested in Pembina will find a great deal to the point about it in the same work.

The weather was fine, the roads were good, and we traveled well till our cattle began to get tender-footed, when we had to go slow. When we reached Mouse [or Souris] river they got so lame that we had to shoe them in some manner or other; so we thought of the iron bands of our trunks, examined the thickest, and with these made shoes which helped us considerably, though they wore out fast, and detained us much on our march. When we arrived on a little river called the Elk Head,[6] Smith and Boller, with their four wagons, left for Berthold.

I kept on with my old guide and Mr. Lemon, with our four wagons, for the Missouri or Fort Stewart. At the last crossing of Mouse river[7] our guide re-

[6] Tête à la Biche of the French is a considerable elevation, now called Moose mountain, off to the N. W. of Larpenteur's present position, giving rise to several tributaries of Mouse river. Two of these were called Tête à la Biche creeks, now known as North Antler and South Antler creeks ; they fall into Mouse river close together, at and near Sourisford, Manitoba, a few miles N. of the U. S. and Canadian boundary. Larpenteur's Elk Head river is one of these—most likely South Antler creek, at Sourisford. If the reader would like to follow Larpenteur in greater detail, he may turn to my Henry and Thompson book, p. 285 and follow-ing of chap. ix. As to the place now in mention by Larpenteur, Henry says on p. 308, "we came to the little river of Tête à la Biche," July 15, 1806. He was then on his way to the Mandans. Smith and Boller, who here leave for Fort Berthold, take a route approximately the same as Henry's, but Larpenteur keeps on westward, to strike the Missouri much higher up.

[7] His first crossing having been at or near Sourisford, as said

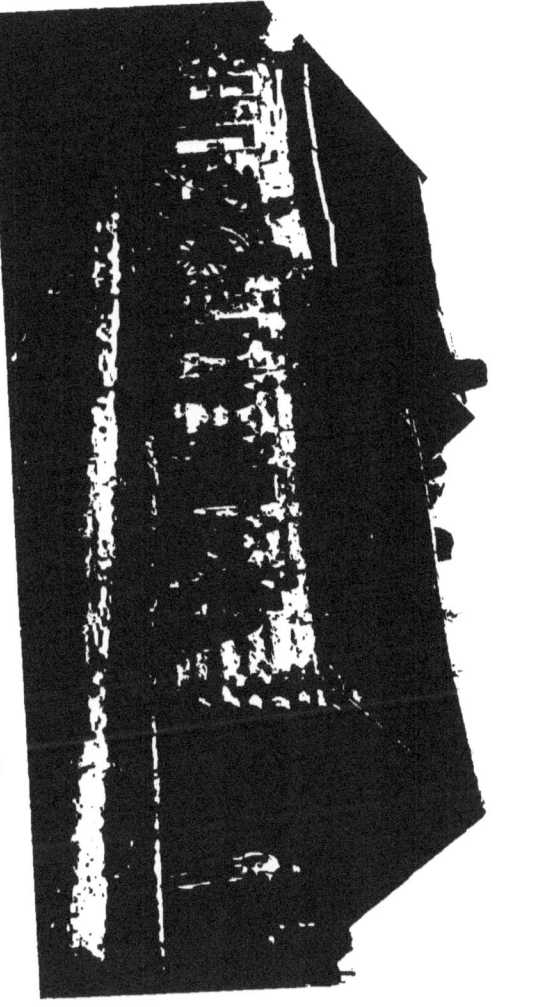

OLD FORT PEMBINA. 1840-84.   NORMAN KITTSON'S TRADING POST.

marked that we had better take on all the dry fire-
wood we could find, as we would not have any more
till we should come near the Bad Lands [Mauvaises
Terres] of the Missouri. Having acted upon his ad-
vice, and done some more shoeing, we again got under way, driving at the rate of about ten miles a day.
On leaving this point our spirits rose, and though we
traveled slowly we still hoped to reach our destination in good time. According to the camps which
our guide could count up, we should not be much
over eight days. Although our guide knew the
way well, he missed one camp. When we neared
the Missouri one evening, the old man, who had gone
ahead, returned to camp saying, " Good news! You
need not spare your firewood; I have seen the Missouri." At this news a cry of joy burst through our
little squad, who threw up their hats and jumped
about like crazy men. Good fires were made, and
in the morning the last stick was burned; we were
glad of it, and left camp fully expecting to reach the
Missouri early. But we were disappointed in that;
we traveled the whole day without wood or water,
and it was dark when we reached a small stream,[10]

in the preceding note, he now strikes Mouse river again,
about Minot, N. Dak., where the G. N. Ry. now crosses it.

[10] Big Muddy creek, already sufficiently indicated in previous
notes. Here Larpenteur is 4½ m. from Fort Stewart.

nearly dry, and without wood, and we had to gather
buffalo chips to make fire.   No Missouri having been
seen, there was great discontentment in camp that
night, for we knew not exactly where we were.   The
old guide was much put out; but, knowing that he
had not been much mistaken, got up early, mounted
his horse, and very soon returned, saying, "Those
who believe that I have not seen the river can come
with me, and I will make them see it."   Thinking we
were lost we had camped within ten miles of Fort
Stewart, which we reached little before sundown on
the 9th of November, 1860, all safe and sound, having lost on the whole journey nothing but one ax,
which we forgot in our camp on Mouse river.

Thus this great journey was performed, being the
first ever made with such wagons.   I had been informed that Fort Kipp,[11] which was within 200 yards
of Fort Stewart, had been burned down by the Indians, but was in hopes to find Fort Stewart still standing.   In this I was disappointed; it had also been
burned, and I found myself obliged to build.   As all
the chimneys of Fort Kipp were still standing, and
this was a great item, I concluded to build on the
same spot, and next day commenced operations.

[11] Little seems to be known of this post, Larpenteur's item concerning which is notable.   It was no doubt named for the James
Kipp already repeatedly mentioned in this work, but no data
regarding its establishment have reached me.

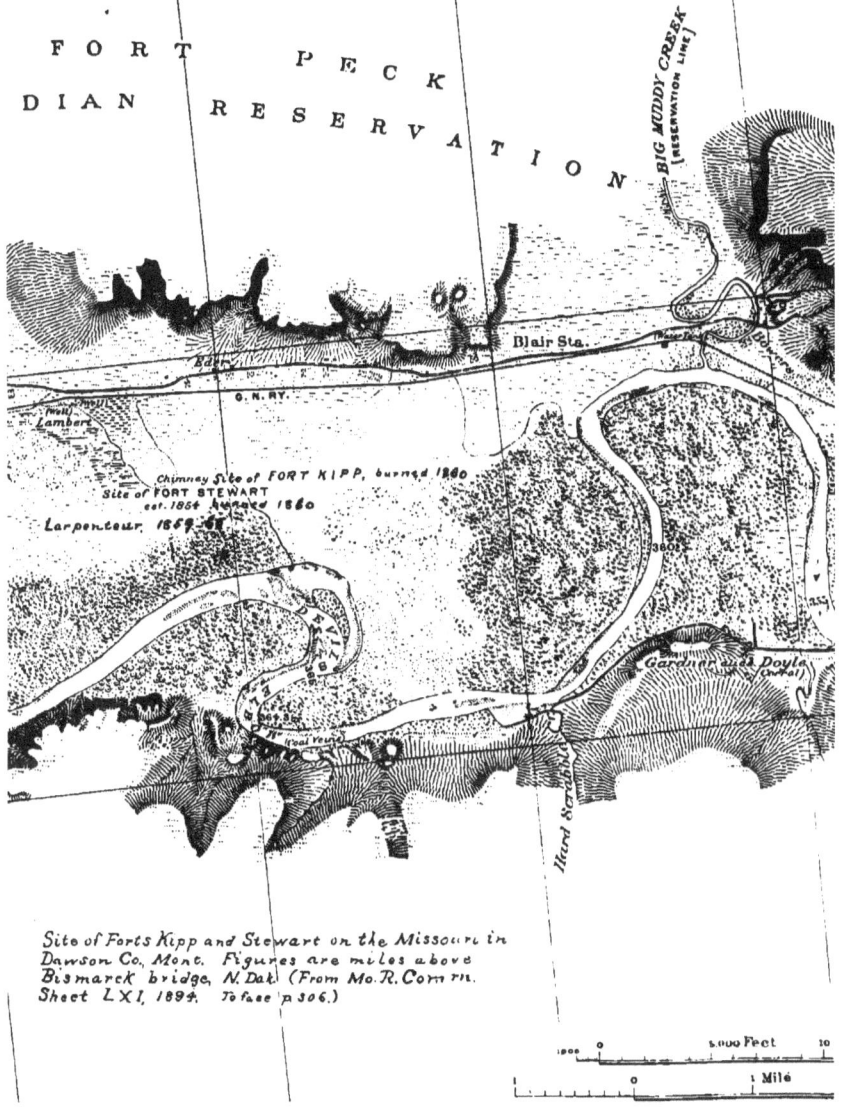

Site of Forts Kipp and Stewart on the Missouri in
Dawson Co., Mont. Figures are miles above
Bismarck bridge, N. Dak. (From Mo. R. Com rn.
Sheet LXI, 1894. To face p 306.)

On the following day two men and one Indian came up from Fort Union. They were much surprised to find me there, and said that Mr. Clark and the Indian agent were on their way up to Poplar river to invite the Crows, who were camped there, to trade at the fort; and that there would be no going out to camps this winter. From this man I learned some particulars of Fort Union. He observed that Clark thought himself a king, being a member of the American Fur Company, in charge of Union, with no opposition, and that he had made himself quite comfortable, but had reduced the men's rations, particularly their biscuits, which had become very small. For his part, he said he was mighty glad I had come, and added, " How glad they will be when they hear that at the fort!"

Clark and the agent, who had taken the ridge road, about two miles back of the fort, came on to our tracks. On examining them, finding that the wheels were iron-bound, they thought that the party could not have been half-breeds, but might have been whiskey peddlers; but as such would have been contrabands, they put spurs to their horses after us. On learning that the agent of the United States was Major Schoonover, whom I knew well, I hoisted a small American flag. On discovering this, they could not make out who we were, but very soon found

out. Clark, on approaching me, turned as pale as a
corpse, saying. " Larpenteur, I'm glad to see you, in
one sense, but, in another, I'm d——d sorry."
Thinking that we might not be acting according to
law, he then remarked, " I presume you are well prepared to carry on trade? " I observed, " The major
already possesses the necessary documents." " All
right, all right! " was his answer. After which he
asked in a light manner, " Would you not like to sell
out? " I replied that I had come to sell to the Indians, not to the Company, and that I thought I could
sell to them to as good advantage as I could to Mr.
Chouteau. Finding that there was no chance to
make a purchase, he observed that he would turn
back immediately, and send men to build at Poplar
river. Knowing that this river was a good place for
Indians to winter, and that it would suit them better
than if I stayed at Fort Kipp, I concluded to abandon
this point, where I had not done much in the way of
building.

My wagons being still loaded, we were under way
again next morning. We had about 25 miles to
make, which we accomplished early next day; and I
don't believe that Lafayette was more cheerfully received in the United States than I was in that camp.
Next day I selected a place for building, and began
operations at once. I was favored by good weather,

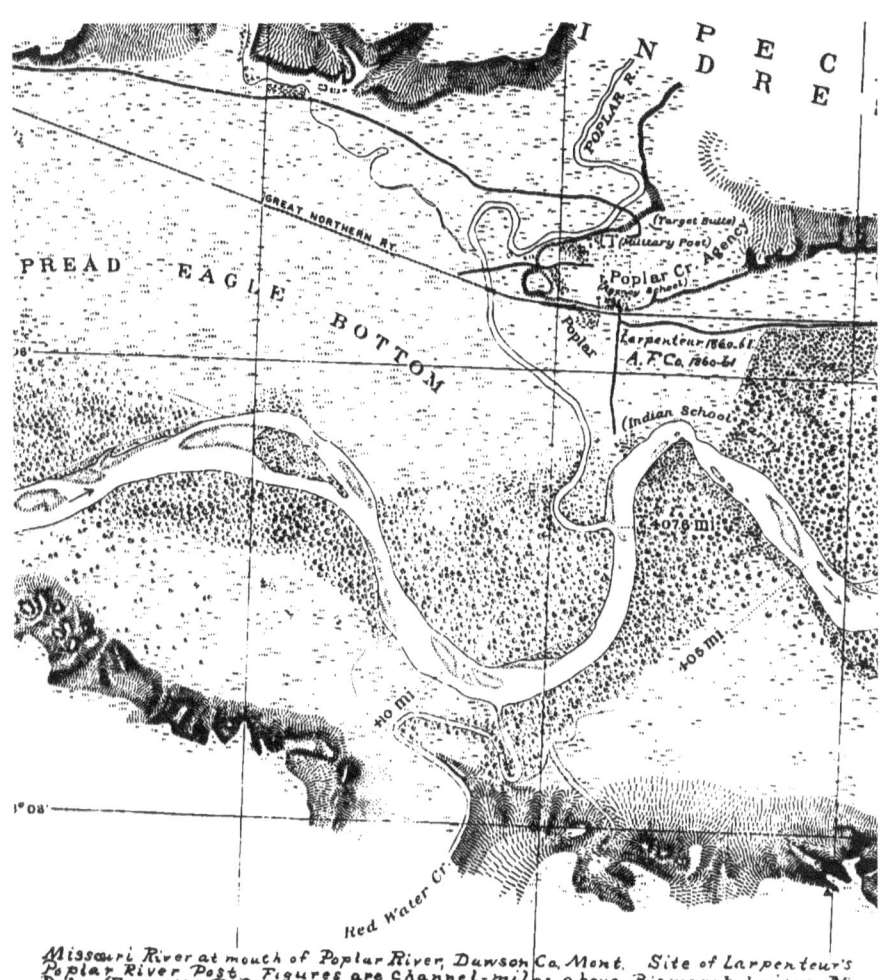

Missouri River at mouth of Poplar River, Dawson Co. Mont. Site of Larpenteur's Poplar River Post. Figures are channel-miles above Bismarck bridge, N. Dak. (From Mo. R. Com'n, Sheet LXII. 1884. To face p. 318.)

and succeeded in building quite a neat little establishment.[12]   In a short time Mr. Clark came here to build, intending to oppose me himself the coming winter [of 1860-61].   I was not sorry for this, for I knew him to be very unpopular with both whites and Indians.

My equipment was not large, but well selected for the Indian trade.   I made a small reduction in prices which satisfied the Indians, and I knew that if I sold out, even at this reduction, I would do well.   This

[12] On left bank of Poplar river near its mouth, no doubt close to where the railroad now crosses, at the eligible site of Poplar sta., Poplar River agency, and the military post of the same name. These situations are practically one, on the high open ground past which the river winds on the N. W. and W. to meander the bottom for 2 or 3 m. to the piece of woodland where it reaches the Missouri.   The very extensive lowland on that side of the Missouri is known as Spread Eagle bottom—all made land in the flood-plain, which was once baked mud before it became solid ground.   The actual position of the mouth of Poplar river has altered by an uncertain number of miles since May 3, 1805, when Lewis and Clark discovered the stream and called it Porcupine river, sailing next day over a part of Spread Eagle bottom.   At that date their Two Thousand Mile creek, now called Redwater, fell into the opposite side of the Missouri only ½ m. above Poplar or Porcupine river; but the mouths of the two streams are now about 2 m. apart by the channel of the Missouri.   The mouth of Poplar river is now 97½ m. by water above that of the Yellowstone ; distance by land from Fort Stewart just the 25 m. Larpenteur gives to the place where he builds ; and this is practically identical with the spot where he had his troubles of 1845 at the Indian camp, as narrated in chap. xii.

gave me the first run of the trade. Clark, in the meantime, had made great calculations on the number of robes the Indians already had in camp, besides the many more they would acquire before the season should be over. He did not think it worth while to make much effort, as he thought also that my four wagon loads could not last long. But he happened to be mistaken in his calculations. Out of my four wagon loads I traded upward of 2,000 robes, besides a great many other skins and hides, and the consequence was that he found himself badly beaten in the spring.

This winter was mild, and it would have been a very pleasant one to me, had it not been for Jeff Smith, who proved to be a sharp trader, and Boller a young blatherskite. They wrote letters to Mr. Lemon against me, even requesting him to keep an eye on me, saying that they believed it was my intention to take my robes around by St. Paul, and cheat them out of that trade, and much more to that effect. As Mr. Lemon was a new hand in the country, he did not know how to take such stuff, which made him look and act quite cross at times. I also received letters from the same parties, in which they used up Lemon about as badly as they did me. Thus matters stood until near spring [1861] when, one day, after a few sharp words, the secret cause of our ill feelings toward each other came out. We then compared letters, upon which everything was explained, the doings of my two partners found out, and harmony re-established between Lemon and myself. I thus found out that Smith had sent two men up to bring down the cattle, to prevent me from taking away the robes. The letter which those men had brought made that request, but I did not wish to risk cattle on that trip, to be stolen or killed by the Sioux, nor did I want to part with them.

Besides putting up my little fort I got all the saw logs I needed to make a large Mackinaw boat, to take down the returns, and also a skiff for Mr. Lemon and Boller to go down as soon as navigation opened. They being the financiers, and myself and Smith the traders, we were to remain at our respective posts till the returns went down. Boller, who was not over 23, and had been but two years in the country,[13] took

[13] Larpenteur is right. It appears from Boller's book, p. 24, that he left St. Louis on the Twilight, Captain John Shaw, May 23, 1858. Larpenteur's name nowhere appears in Boller, and I have failed to find any passages referring to the visit of which Larpenteur speaks. Boller was up the river once, but gives the date as 1863. It is obvious from Boller's silence and Larpenteur's compliments that the two men fell out ; but with their quarrel the editor has no concern, though he has taken the liberty to mitigate his author's severity. Mr. Boller's present address is 110 Sherman Avenue, Denver, Col. According to Chittenden, Rep. 1897, p. 3890, the Twilight was a side-wheeler, 160 x 32 feet,

it upon himself to write long letters from Berthold
about what I was to do and not to do, and, above all,
warned me not to be extravagant in building—as
though I had just come into the country!

As I had not sent the cattle down, Smith concluded
to send Boller up to see how matters stood. About
the middle of March [1861] Boller arrived, and, as it
was at night, he had to knock at the door of my extravagant improvements. His supper for himself and
man was gotten up, and then it was so late that little was said. In the morning I showed him my store
and warehouse, both full f robes, all my fine logs,
timber to make the skiff, about which he had written
to me so often, and also the cattle, which were in first-
rate order for the time of the year, remarking at the
same time, " They will do first-rate to take a trip to
St. Paul." After I had showed him the establishment inside and out, at which I saw he was astonished and pleased, particularly at the sight of the pile
of robes, I remarked, " Do you think I have been extravagant? I have scarcely room enough." To
which he replied, " I am really surprised. You are
well fixed here. We live more like hogs than like
people with old Jeff Smith, and I have had a mighty

in the mountain trade, snagged Sept., 1865, opp. mouth of Fire
creek, in the bend of that name, ⅓ m. above Napoleon, Lafayette
Co., Mo.

HENRY A. BOLLER IN INDIAN DRESS, 1862 63.

disagreeable winter of it." I then asked, "What were all those letters written for—that one, in particular, about my taking the robes and peltries to St. Paul, to cheat you two gentlemen out of them? All you see here belong to Robert Campbell till we have a settlement with him; after which, if there is anything to divide among ourselves, each will get his share. Every hair of this goes to St. Louis, not to St. Paul." All his reply was " Let us bury the hatchet."

The river was ready for navigation on the 3d of April [1861], and on the 5th the two great financiers departed for St. Louis. On their arrival at Berthold Mr. Smith, instead of remaining at his post like myself, got in the skiff and went to St. Louis. Mr. Campbell, astonished to see him, asked what brought him down. Not liking the reception he was given by Mr. Campbell, or from some other cause, he went to Mr. Chouteau. Mr. Lemon, who could not get a steamer with an outfit, as he had expected, was obliged to go up again, to assist in bringing down our returns. Not knowing that Smith had hired to Chouteau, Lemon looked for him in all such places as those where he generally kept himself, but Smith could not be found. He had gone up to some place on the river with the intention of returning to Berthold with Mr. Chouteau. Mr. Lemon made arrangements with Mr. Chouteau to take passage with him, and also to bring down our returns.

On the 19th of June, 1861, we learned by an Indian who came from Union that Mr. Chouteau had arrived there with two steamers, and, on making further inquiries, found that Mr. Lemon was on board one of them. The second day after that an individual by the name of Louis Dauphin—a renowned hunter —made his appearance, and from him I learned that Mr. Lemon was coming up on the Chippewa, that the other steamer, the Spread Eagle, had turned back from Union, and that the Chippewa would be up this far to-morrow or next day. On reaching Dauphin houses,[14] about six miles below my place by land, but double that distance by water, Mr. Lemon got off to come ahead of the boat to give me the news. After the greetings usual on such arrivals were passed, he remarked: " Larpenteur, I have bad news to give you.

[14] Of Dauphin's post I know nothing further than that 6 m. by land below Larpenteur's place on Poplar river is the distance thence to the Indian village of Deer Tail, on the N. bank of the Missouri, where the river washes a low bluff 1 m. S. of the railroad, 3 m. from Brockton sta. The Spread Eagle above said is no doubt the boat for which the bottom described in note [11] was named. She met the usual fate of Missouri boats in being snagged. This happened in Pinckney bend, a place at the foot of Berger or Shepherd bottom, opp. Pinckney, Warren Co., Mo., a year or two after the date in the text. For the Chippewa, see next note.

In the first place, I came up with Mr. Chouteau, having made arrangements with him to take down our returns, but the boat is burned up. I had been off her but little while when I saw her all on fire, and immediately heard the report of the explosion. In the second place, war is declared; the United States are in a great revolution, and there is no sale for anything. In the third place, old Smith has deserted us, and won't let us have his robes. I have other news, but I hate to tell it to you." On my insisting, he said, " All your improvements are burned down. Your house caught fire in the middle of the night, and not even a stitch of clothing was saved." On saying this he paused, and I exclaimed, " Is there any more? " "Is that not enough?" said he. " Yes." I replied, "it is more than enough to lose my home at Little Sioux. But it is no use to cry over spilt milk, and it is under such circumstances that a man is tried."

It was a little before sunset when Lemon arrived, and just at dark we learned the particulars of the accident. The boat was set on fire by one of the hands, who had gone down into the hold to steal liquor. Some of it having run upon his clothes while he was drawing it the candle came in contact with the wet parts and ignited them. He was burned badly, and then the boat took fire. Immediately upon the alarm being given the boat was landed, and she was abandoned as soon as all passengers and hands were ashore. Nothing could be saved for fear of an explosion of the magazine, in which there was a great quantity of powder. After being abandoned she drifted about two miles, and then exploded on the south side of the river.[15] Owing to this accident we sold our cattle and wagons to very good advantage to some gentlemen who resided in Bitterroot Valley, one of them a merchant named Warren, and others going to the Columbia.

Not expecting any steamer to take down our returns I had pushed work on the boat so well that, six days after Lemon's arrival, it was completed; she was 65 feet in length and 11 feet in breadth of beam, be-

[15] "At 8 A. M. passed the place where the Chippewa was burned. At 10 A. M. opposite Poplar River," Harkness, Diary, Cont. Mont. Hist. Soc. ii, 1896, p. 347, at date of Monday, June 9, 1862. The Chippewa was the first boat that ever passed above the mouth of Maria's river to Fort Brulé (McKenzie or Piegan: note ⁴, p. 111), which she reached in 1859 (July 17), and shared with the Key West in 1860 (July 2) the honor of first reaching Benton itself. She was a stern-wheeler of 160 x 32 feet, owned by the A. F. Co., W. H. Humphreys, master, at the time of the disaster which Larpenteur relates. This occurred on the evening of Sunday, June 23, 1861—not in "May," as given by Chittenden, Rep., p. 3876. The place where she burned, about 15 m. by water below Poplar river, became locally known as Disaster Bend. The liquor on board was being smuggled; the lawful freight included other goods for the A. F. Co., Indian annuities, and about 25 kegs of powder. No lives were lost.

ing thus large enough to take my returns and those
of Smith. The bursting of the Chippewa set my men
almost crazy, thinking they would get a fortune out
of the wreckage. They did not like the idea of rowing
my boat down, although they were engaged to do so;
and besides, they feared the draft, on account of the
rebellion in the United States. I was therefore forced
to give $100 for the trip. I had engaged a pilot for
$300, but he at last refused to go. At last I suc-
ceeded in getting a crew, consisting of four to row and
one pilot, and on the 2d of July, 1861, we left Poplar
river. On the fourth day after our departure we
reached Union. At the same time Mr. Rider came
from Berthold with two of our wagons and four yoke
of our cattle, Jeff Smith having made some arrange-
ment with the company. This accounted for his having sent for the cattle I had; for he wanted to dispose
of them to his own private interest. Mr. Lemon having demanded pay for the cattle, a check on Mr.
Chouteau for the amount agreed upon was given,
which was so much saved. Smith had no idea that
we would fall in with the cattle where we did.

We remained at Union about two hours, and
pushed off again. On the fourth day out from this
place we landed at Berthold. We called on Smith
for the robes, but failed, after all our efforts, having
been able to get nothing more than the buffalo

tongues. Without any accident we went on well, and a little below Nebraska City met the steamer Emilie,[16] Captain Nicholas Wall, bound for Omaha. We made arrangements with him to take down our robes, and waited for his return. It was still considered dangerous to travel down the river, though not nearly so much so as it had been, and when the boat returned there was a company of soldiers on board from Omaha, bound for St. Louis; but no bushwhackers were seen, and on the 4th of August we . reached the port of St. Louis, all safe.

[16] I have no means of identifying this Emilie, the name having been borne by three or four different boats. One of them gave name to Emilie Bend of the Missouri, where she was snagged in 1842, about halfway between Pinckney and Washington, Mo. She was a packet owned in part by P. Chouteau and Co. Emilie No. 2, owned by the Hannibal and St. Jo. R. R., wrecked at St. Joseph, Mo., in 1865, is said to have been the first side-wheeler that ever reached Benton, and is very likely the boat Larpenteur means. Capt. Nicholas Wall is the person for whom Nick Wall bar and point are named. The bar is situated in a bend at the upper part of Spread Eagle bottom, 10 m. by water above the mouth of Poplar river. If the reader will turn to Lewis and Clark, ed. of 1893, p. 295, he will find that on May 4, 1805, the explorers " passed a small creek in a deep bend on the south, with a sand-island opposite it." This sand-island is Nick Wall bar; the creek is now called Antelope creek—the same that Clark's map of 1814 marks an Indian fort at the mouth of. Nick Wall point is the great tongue of land that makes Marion bend, near Chelsea sta. This bend has grown immensely since 1805, for L. and C. sailed right across Nick Wall point from the little creek just said, on a course of 3 m. N. 10° W.

CHAPTER XVII.

(1861-63.)

As Mr. Lemon had reported, there was no sale for robes. The best part of our robes had been stolen. No longer had I a house to live in. Now what to do? Mr. Campbell, who saw what a plight we were in, said, "Gentlemen, I cannot sell your robes, except at a great sacrifice, which I see no necessity to make. If you wish to return I will furnish your outfit. Now make up your minds and let me know." Having consulted upon what to do we made up our minds to return. Smith, of course, was out; we allowed Boller a small share, but he was to remain out of the country.

Our outfit was soon ready and shipped again by St. Paul, where we bought our cattle. This time we adopted Burbank's way of freighting. We bought light wagons and put but one yoke to each. In this way one man can drive two wagons, and it is no trouble to get through swampy places, as each wagon takes only from 18 to 20 hundredweight.

We left St. Paul on the 14th of September [1861], with seven wagons and eight men, bound for Poplar river. We traveled well, but I was so sick most of the way that it was feared at one time I was going to leave my bones in the prairie. The weather was also very disagreeable. The previous trip I walked the whole way, nearly 900 miles, except two days; but this time I rode more than half the time. We went pretty nearly the same route; the only difference was that we struck direct for St. Joseph instead of Pembina. We had provided ourselves with ox shoes, and got our cattle shod on arriving there. I got another first-rate guide, by the name of Louison Vallée. This guide was one of the best hunters I ever saw for buffalo, as well as for small game; he was near fifty, about six feet three, built in proportion, a very powerful man, and a tremendous walker. He made us live on ducks and geese at the start, and, when we got in among buffalo, on the fat of the land. His killing so many fine fat ducks I believe saved my life. In coming in with a load of ducks he would exclaim: " Monsieur Larpenteur, c'est bon pour la moustache," for he could not speak English. He was as good a guide as my first one; he took us farther north, but managed to get us through without seeing Indians, except the day previous to our arrival.

When we came near the Missouri he observed that

he had never been up to Poplar river; he could put
us on the Missouri, but not take us direct to the spot.
That did not make much difference with us, as we had
a man by the name of Joseph Ramsay,[1] who had been
the hunter for Fort Union for 20 years, and said he

[1] Corruption of his Spanish name, which I suppose would be
correctly written José Ramusio. He figures in Boller, p. 373 :
" John Wallace was the principal hunter since old *José Ramisie*
had lost one of his hands by the bursting of his gun. Previous
to that accident José was one of the very best ' runners ' in that
part of the country. Wallace was brave even to foolhardiness,
and the following spring paid the penalty of his rashness with
his life." Dr. Matthews supplies the following note :

" Ramsay was a corruption of his true name, which I never
learned. I saw him once in the spring of 1871, in very cold, unpleasant weather, when I was on a scout from Fort Buford to
Fort Peck. One day near the mouth of Poplar river, as we were
passing a small cluster of Assiniboine teepees, which stood 100
or 200 yards off our trail, a number of the Indians turned out to
look at our party. Some old pioneer among us cried out,
'There's Joe Ramsay. I must go and see him.' As I had often
heard of Ramsay, and was curious to see him, I turned aside
from the trail also. I found him a tall, good-looking old man
of Spanish type. He spoke English very imperfectly. He was
dressed like an Indian, wrapped in a blanket, and wore no hat.
He had lost his right arm. I learned afterward that his case was
something like that of John Brazeau, of which I have already
told you. When he lost his arm, and could no longer earn a living in the Fur Company, he was turned out or at least made so
unwelcome that he left. Then he found refuge among the Indians, who fed him till he died. At the time I met him, he was
living on the charity of the Assiniboines, although they were
themselves in a half-starving condition."

knew the country well.   So the remainder of the journey was left to Ramsay.   We did not, at the time,
consider ourselves more than two days' travel from
our destination.   In the morning Ramsay took the
lead, and the guide went ahead of the teams, in his
own direction toward the Missouri, expecting to fall
in with us from time to time.   I remained with Ram-
sey, going ahead of the teams.   After traveling about
an hour I observed that I thought he was going too
far north.   " No," said he, " I am on the direct way.
You see that big hill yonder, with that pile of rocks
on it?   From there you can see the Missouri."
When we came near the hill, being anxious to see the
Missouri, and, at the same time, thinking that my
man was lost, I started ahead of him.   But, when I
reached the top of the hill, the Missouri was not to be
seen, nor any sign of it.   As Ramsay came up I asked
him to show me the Missouri.   He looked around,
very much surprised, not knowing what to say, and I
saw plainly that he was lost.   I then pointed out a
direction, went back to the wagons, and changed our
course.   We had gone but a little way when we saw
an Indian coming after us at full gallop.   On approaching us he asked: " Are you going to Woody
Mountain? "   Ramsay had taken quite a northerly
direction.

This Indian was Broken Arm, the chief of the

Canoe band of Assiniboines; he said that they had
come across our tracks, and made sure whose they
were. Many of his people wanted to follow him, but
he did not allow them to do so, as he knew I would
not like it. He then asked me where I was going to
winter. I told him at my former place. He remarked that it was not so suitable as Fort Stewart,
where all his band intended to winter; that I had better change my plans; that there were no Indians as yet
on the Missouri, but they would all come to my place
as soon as they should learn that I had arrived. This
was all a lie, for I found out afterward that most of
the Assiniboines were at Fort Charles,[2] about 50 miles
by land above Fort Stewart.

[2] Fort Charles stood on the N. bank of the Missouri, in the
vicinity of Macon and Wolf Point stations of the G. N. Ry., below
Wolf creek from the N. and Elk Prairie creek from the S. The
latter is Lackwater or Little Dry creek of Lewis and Clark, the
next one below their Big Dry creek, which latter is the one
wrongly marked Elk Prairie creek on various maps : see L.
and C., ed. of 1893, p. 299, where the G. L. O. map misled me.
Fort Charles was built on the first point from the N. below this
Little Dry or Elk Prairie creek, about 3 m. S. S. W. of Macon
sta., at about 124 channel-miles above the mouth of the Yellowstone, and about 26½ of the same above present mouth of Poplar
river. The point is now 4 m. below the mouth of the creek; but
the position of the latter is altogether different from what it used
to be, in consequence of the remarkable Fort Charles cut-off. On
May 5, 1805, Lewis and Clark sailed 5 m. due S. into this cut-off
from the bluffs on the N. side where Calf creek comes into the

Owing to his report I consented to go to Fort Stewart; the Indian guided us, saying we would get there the next day. It was late at night when our guide Vallée came to the camp, quite angry with Ramsay. It snowed that night about four inches, and kept quite cold all the next forenoon, but moderated in the afternoon. A little before sunset we were at Fort Stewart, strange to say, again on the same date as last year—the 9th of November, 1861.

It was a glad set of men who put up the lodge, not to be taken down till comfortable quarters were made; and, after a bouncing supper, we turned in, with the pleasant idea that there would be no hitching up in the morning. Had Ramsay taken us in the right direction, we should have reached Poplar river the day the Indian overtook us, and found good quarters already built. My own had been burned down, but

bottom. They thus went at a right angle across the present channel of the Missouri, which is flowing from W. to E., and camped under the bluffs on the S. side. Next morning they went S. 30° W. 1½ m. to the mouth of their Little Dry creek, issuing from a gorge between two bluffs directly into the Missouri, which then washed those bluffs. This old channel is the Fort Charles cut-off, the upper arm of which is now closed up, while the open lower arm carries Elk Prairie creek some 3 m. N. through the bottom to the point where it now strikes the channel of the Missouri almost opp. Wolf Point sta., 2 m. below Wolf creek, and 1½ m. above the Calf creek just mentioned. The whole formation is a typical case of its kind.

those of Clark were still up, and would have saved us a great deal of disagreeable labor.

On rising in the morning we found about five inches of snow on the ground, and it was still snowing; but the wind soon changed and a cold northwester made it impossible to work. From this time until March [1862] extremely cold weather continued. Through the assistance of squaws whom I employed to heat water and daub the houses, we succeeded in getting ourselves comfortable quarters, but no stockade. I made use of the places we prepared the previous fall. Buffalo were so plentiful here last summer that they ate up all the grass; it looked as though fire had burned the prairies. In consequence of this and the hard winter [of 1861-62] I lost all my cattle—20 head. Owing to the severity of this winter my trade was light, after that of the Assiniboines was over. I had but 1,000 robes, a great many goods left on hand, and more trade must be made. I knew the Gros Ventres of the Prairie[3] were at war with the Blackfeet—that is, with the Piegans; that they dared not go to Benton; that few traders had been in their camp; and, consequently, that they must have yet a great many robes.

[3] Not the Grosventres of the Missouri, who lived with the Mandans, but the Atsinas or Fall Indians, a tribe of Algonquian stock, usually confederated with the Blackfeet or Siksikas. See a previous note.

Matters standing thus, I proposed to Lemon to go after the Gros Ventres. I had a man in view for this trip who knew the country, and intended to send him with Lemon. After a great deal of persuasion Lemon agreed to go. My man, whose name was Louis El,[4] was ready. My instructions to Lemon were, in the first place, to do all he could to bring the Indians down with their robes; and, secondly, if he could not succeed in that, to get enough of them to come with what number of horses would be required to take all my goods up to Milk river at Dauphin's[5]

[4] So Larpenteur spells the name, which is Louis Elle in Boller, p. 366, etc.

[5] " Stopped at Dauphan's cabin, eight miles [by river] below Milk River. Traded for robes, etc., and took him to Milk River," Diary of James Harkness, June 10, 1862, aboard the Emilie, in Cont. Mont. Hist. Soc. ii, 1896, p. 348. The cabin was in the vicinity of Little Porcupine creek, 1 m. E. of which, 3 m. from its mouth, is Lenox sta. of the G. N. Ry. This is near where Larpenteur intended to summer, if not the same spot, and 8 m. below Milk river is exactly the situation of Lewis and Clark's " Gulf in the Island Bend," no trace of which remains. But it here appears, and beyond, p. 342, that Dauphin's " old fort," of which Larpenteur speaks, was *at* the mouth of Mill river. I am uncertain whether this Dauphin was Louis, the famous hunter mentioned on p. 324. No doubt there were more than one person of the name, which varies to Dauphine, Dauphiné, Dauphiny, etc.; but this individual is most probably the one for whom Dauphin rapids were named—the first bad ones below Judith river. " We passed several rapids, one of which was called Dauphin Rapid, after one of our engagés, who had fallen

old fort, where I intended to remain during the summer, and where I would have a boat ready for him to go down with what returns I should have; but by all means to do his best to bring them down with robes.

Under those instructions and conditions they started afoot, with their rifles on their shoulders and a dog to carry or drag their sugar and coffee, about the 10th of May [1862].

In the meantime I set to work on my boat, which went very slowly, as I was out of provisions and had neither horse nor mule to send after meat. I had traded a horse and a mule, but one Mr. Assiniboine had relieved me of both; and I had to send my men with the cart after meat, when it was not killed too far from the establishment, or to pack it on their backs.

Twelve days after Lemon's departure he returned with a trading party of Gros Ventres, having 450 robes. After this trade was over, I proposed to put my plan into execution; but Lemon objected, saying that the Indians would rob me of all my goods, and that we had better go down together. As he had been quite contrary all winter, and fretful at every

into the river at this place," Maxim., Trav. of 1833, ed. of 1843, p. 230. I shot those rapids in 1874, and felt much better after than before taking them, in a small open boat. See Lewis and Clark, ed. of 1893, pp. 329, 330.

little disappointment, I became dissatisfied with him, and determined to have nothing more to do with him. So I went on preparing to go down stream. On the 4th of June [1862], we were ready to start, with oars all shipped, when a steamer hove in sight. We awaited her arrival, and found she was the Shreveport, Captain John La Barge,[6] who informed us that his brother Joseph was not far behind, coming up with the Emilie, and that he had letters for us from Robert Campbell, also some provisions. When we were ready to push off, he asked us if we had any ice. I told him that he would find some in a barrel. The ice had been so thick that a large cake of it, which we had covered in the sand, had kept until this time. The steamer resumed its way up, and we made our oars play down stream. We learned by John La Barge that they had formed a company to oppose the American Fur Company, the firm being La Barge, Harkness, and Co.[7] We met the Emilie about 20

[6] There were several others of this name, one of them Robert La Barge. Captain Joseph La Barge still (1898) lives in St. Louis, at a very advanced age. In 1843 he was pilot of the Omega, on which Audubon's party went from St. Louis to Fort Union : see my note in Aud. and his Journs., i, 1897, p. 492. The Emilie was his property. Captain John La Barge had just rung the bell of the Helena to make a landing opposite Bismarck, N. Dak., when he dropped dead at the wheel, May 1, 1885.

[7] The firm of La Barge, Harkness, and Co. was formed at St. Louis in the spring of 1862. The partners were Eugene Jaccard,

miles below Big Muddy river.[8]   By the letter from
Mr. Campbell we learned that robes and all furs and
peltries had risen in price, and also that he had sent
us groceries of all kinds, as Captain John La Barge
had already informed us.   I was sorry that Lemon
had not consented to let me take my goods up to
Milk river; had he done so, I should have found myself well supplied, and we would have done well in
that country.   But, as a large company was now organized to oppose the American Fur Company, I did

James Harkness, Joseph La Barge, John La Barge, and William (?)
Galpin.   Each partner is said to have put in $10,000 ; the steam-
ers Shreveport and Emilie were purchased ; the former left St.
Louis April 30, and the latter May 10, 1862, in charge of the two
Captains La Barge, respectively.   On the Emilie was Mr. Harkness, whose Diary of the trip occupies Cont. Mont. Hist. Soc. ii,
1896, pp. 343–361.   They landed at Fort Benton at noon of Tuesday, June 17 : "had a business meeting of all the partners and
decided to build our post a mile and a half above Fort Benton
naming it Fort La Barge," *ibid.*, p. 349.   Again, p. 350, date of
June 28 : " Laid out Fort La Barge, three hundred by two hundred feet.   Madam La Barge drove the first stake and my daughter, Margaret, the second."   They also made a post near Fort
Pierre on this trip ; for we read, at date of Sept. 20, " found
ourselves within one-half mile of our new post, just above Fort
Pierre.   Staid two hours with Lapambois [La Framboise]. . .
his house is the best and goods in better order than any," *ibid.*, p.
359.

    [8] On Saturday, June 7, 1862.   " Met R. Lemon and Larpenter
two days out, and took the latter back with us," says Harkness,
Diary, p. 347.

not think it advisable to return with the boat, though
I could have done so at but little expense, and most
likely would have done so, if Lemon had been the
right kind of a man. Taking everything into consideration, I thought best sell out.

So we sold out to Joseph La Barge. Mr. Lemon
went on down to Berthold with the boat to deliver
the goods, and await the return of the Emilie. I
turned back with Captain La Barge, under a pro-
visional understanding, to examine and select a point
to build near the mouth of Milk river. Having examined that vicinity, I chose a situation at the head
of Moose Point,⁹ about 10 miles above Milk river by
land and 15 by the Missouri.

⁹ We hear of Larpenteur at this place in Harkness' Diary,
p. 356. While at Fort La Barge Harkness built a boat 40 feet
long, 7½ beam, christened her the Maggie, no doubt for his
daughter Margaret, launched her on Aug. 26, 1862, and started
down river next day. On Friday, Sept. 5, he says : " Off at
3.30, passed Dry Creek at 5.30, and arrived at Dauphan's at
11.30. . . Chambers, Larpenter, Lemon and the men all well."
I believe that Larpenteur's Moose point is the same as El Paso
point of Stevens' map—the very bold headland on the E. and S.
around which the Missouri makes such a sweep for a few miles
above Milk river. A part of this sweep, where the river is flowing
N. for about 5 m. before it rounds to the E., is El Paso—a Spanish
name, reminding us of the far away Rio Grande. There the
bluffs on each hand are not over a mile apart. This strait-
ened place is The Pass, from the exit of which the flood plain
speedily widens to 2-2⅔ m. as it approaches Milk river, where the
joint bottom of the two streams is fully 4 m. wide. At the head

I remained there until the return of the Emilie from Benton, when I again got on board, bound for St. Louis. At Berthold we took on our robes and proceeded. At Fort Pierre we learned that Smith, who had gone down with his robes in a small Mackinaw, had returned with Mr. Chouteau, whom he had met a little below, and had left his robes at Fort Pierre, in charge of Mr. Charles Primeau. Mr. Lemon demanded them as our property. Mr. Primeau consented to give them up on our paying him $50 for storage. We gave the required amount, and took them on board the Emilie. So we got out our robes at last, though, from what we learned afterward, we supposed Smith had sold them to Mr. Chouteau. They both felt very much surprised, on their return to Fort Pierre, to find the robes gone.

of the pass the Big Dry river of Lewis and Clark falls into the bight of a deep bend on the S., 2½ m. below Fort Peck; it still bears the name it originally received on May 9, 1805. At the foot of the pass Larpenteur founded the post he calls Fort Galpin, on the left bank, N. side, of the Missouri, directly opposite Moose or El Paso point. The situation is now only 12½ m. by the channel above Milk river, instead of the 15 m. Larpenteur gives. The bends seem to have contracted of late years, and are certainly much shorter than they were when Lewis and Clark went through. Fort Peck was flourishing in 1874, when I was there, but has since been abandoned. Galpin continues to be the place of a small settlement which goes by the original name. From Galpin up to the site of Peck, on the same side of the river, is less than 4 m. by land, but by water about 8½ m.

Early in July [1862] we reached St. Louis, where, after a final settlement, I found myself with $1,400, from our dividends. This was my all, after two years of hard work, trouble, and exposure. Having made arrangements with the firm of La Barge and Co., which was to give me one-fourth of the net proceeds of the Assiniboine and Gros Ventres of the Prairie trade, I left for my place at Little Sioux.

On arrival I found my family all well, but living in a very poor log house, which was standing about 40 steps from my main buildings, and had escaped the fire. All I could see of my improvements, which had cost me upward of $3,000, was a pile of ashes; and I had no insurance.

I went the rounds at once, settled all my debts, big and small, and eight days afterward was again under way for the upper country, having shipped at Sioux City, on the Shreveport, bound for Benton, with goods for the Indian trade.

Late in August [1862] we reached Milk river, when the Missouri became so low that the steamer could proceed no further. The next day, while we were taking the goods into Dauphin fort, a large war party of Sioux gave us a few shots, and stole several head of horses from the Crows. The Shreveport left, and I remained in Dauphin until teams came from Benton to take up what goods the company had for that place, and also to move me up to the fort, which I called Galpin.[10]   On our way up we left Owen McKenzie about 150 miles below this point, to build a trading post for the Assiniboines.

Here I erected a handsome, good little fort, and might have had a pleasant time.   But in consequence of the very mild winter we had no buffalo, and the Indians, who were starving as well as ourselves, became very unruly.   At one time they threatened to pillage my stores, and · for a while our case looked rather dark; but they contented themselves with

[10] In honor of Charles E. Galpin, of whom Dr. Matthews writes to me as follows :   " He was called ' Major ' Galpin, but I never knew why.   Perhaps he was once an Indian agent—all Indian agents were dubbed Major in those days ; perhaps he had belonged to a militia regiment: but most likely the title was a sort of ' Kentucky brevet.'   I have heard that when he was well on in his cups, he used to introduce himself to the whole world as ' Major Galpin of Dakota, a gentleman of the old school.'   He must have been a long time in the country.   I met him twice ; once at Fort Berthold, in 1865, when he was in the Indian trade, and once at Fort Rice, in 1868, when he kept a sutler store and did some Indian trade.   From Fort Rice he went to one of the then newly established agencies—Grand River, I think—where he died about 1870.   He was a tall, fine-looking man of good presence and had evidently had good early advantages.   He was married to a Sioux woman of unusually fine character, and by her had several children, all of whom I think are dead.   In Dr. F. V. Hayden's Indian Tribes of the Missouri Valley, in Trans. Amer. Philos. Soc., there is a picture of her (fig. 4), with one of her children on her knee, and a flattering notice of her on p. 457."

stealing a few articles. I tried my men, but they refused to fight, saying they would rather let the Indians take all the goods than expose their own lives. I
had a mean, cowardly set of men, many of whom had
been hired by Captain John La Barge on his return
from Benton, during his first trip. I knew them of
old, and had I had my own way about this, they
should never have been in my employment.

   In spite of all this my trade was tolerably fair this
winter [1862-63]. McKenzie did little. Early in the
fall he had a fight with the Sioux, in which one man
was killed, besides one Assiniboine and several horses.
This was a party of about 200 warriors, who attacked
our men in their house. The latter immediately cut
portholes, and defended themselves through them.
Our man was killed in the house by a ball which penetrated the door. The Indians were bold enough to
come and shoot through the portholes; but one of
them remained there. The fight lasted all day; there
were but four white men and six Assiniboines on our
side. The next day three Sioux were found dead,
and there were signs of several wounded ones, who
had been taken away. This fight frightened the Assiniboines away from the post, and was the cause why
McKenzie did but little trade—only 350 robes.

   Toward spring [1863] we were in a starving condition, game of all kinds extremely scarce, and men

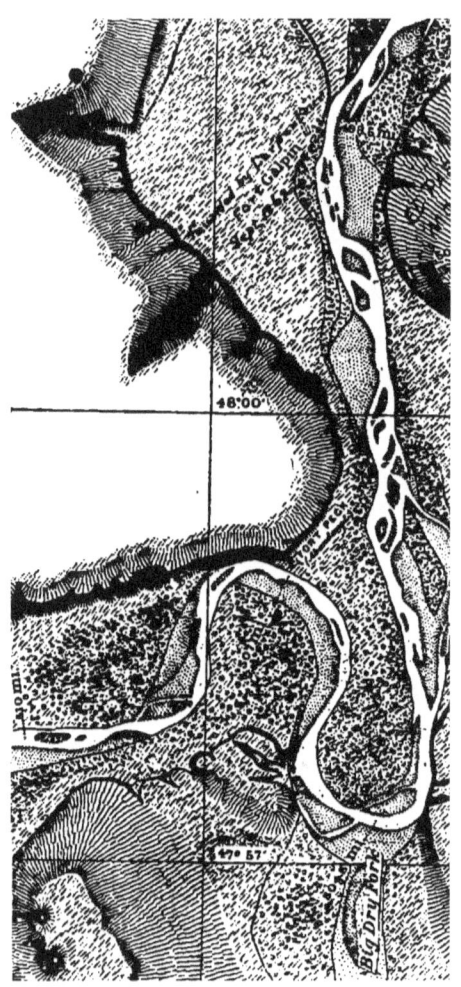

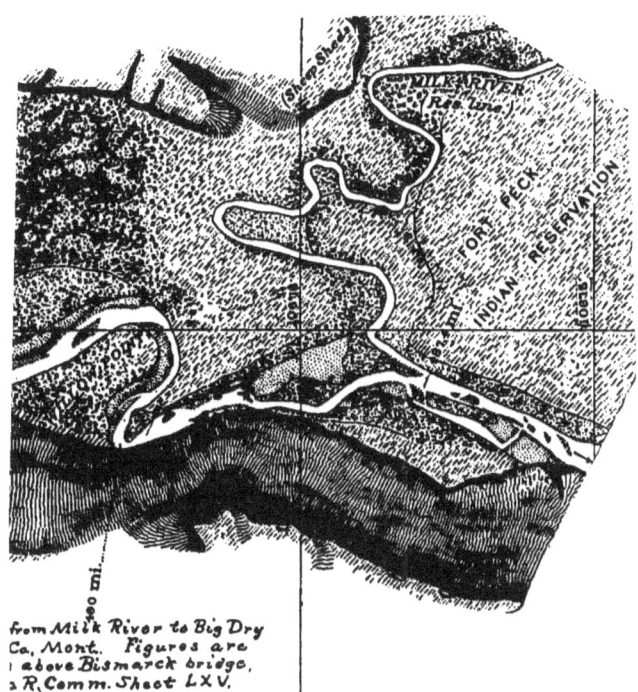

from Milk River to Big Dry
Co. Mont. Figures are
above Bismarck bridge,
R. Comm. Sheet LXV.

afraid to go out for a hunt. For about six weeks I lived on nothing but jerked elk meat, having some salt but being entirely out of other groceries. There is little substance in elk meat. I became so weak that I could scarcely get up the river bank with a bucket of water; my knees felt like giving way. It was only by seeking for coffee in the warehouse, picking it up grain by grain out of the dirt, that I now and then got a cup of coffee, without sugar; but it was a great treat notwithstanding.

On the 11th of June, 1863, Capain John La Barge landed at this place, bound again for Benton, or, rather, for Fort La Barge,[11] which the firm had built in opposition to Benton. Having heard some great stories, all of which he or they believed, previous to seeing me, the firm had made up their minds to discharge me. In consequence of this they abandoned Owen McKenzie's post and brought him up to take charge of Fort Galpin. McKenzie was a great drunkard, not at all fit to be in charge of such an establishment; but, without any inquiries, my charge was made over to him. Captain La Barge, not satisfied with this, and being the meanest man I ever

[11] As we have already seen note ¹, p. 339. As in the instance of Mr. Boller, Larpenteur proceeds to severe strictures upon the Captains La Barge. I am sorry for this, as I believe him to be too harsh. But he is entitled to the expression of his opinions, which it is not my part to confirm or confute.

worked for, except his brother, told some of the men
that I had given him a very bad account of their behavior. This set them against me; and now that
I was no longer in charge, one gentleman among
them—a bully nearly six feet six inches tall—took it
into his head one fine day to give me a pounding.
He would have done so had it not been for my son,
who was about 20 years of age,[12] and much of a man.
He saw me in a quarrel, and, thinking that there
would be a fight, went into the house, and got his rifle.
By that time we were engaged in the fight. I received a severe blow, which stunned me; and when I
recovered I saw my antagonist lying as if dead at my
feet. I made sure it was none of my doing, and next
saw my son in the act of giving him another blow,
saying, " Let me kill the son of a b——h." McKenzie, who had come up, said, " Don't strike him again,
Charles; you have killed him." During all this time
the men were standing outside near their houses, not
daring to approach, and when we left him they came
and took him in for dead; but he recovered.

McKenzie now being in charge, my presence was
no longer needed at this place. I got a canoe, and,
taking my son and a young freeman named Keiser,
went down to meet Captain Joseph La Barge, who
was coming up with the steamer Robert Campbell,

[12] Having been born Aug. 9, 1842 : see that date, p. 175.

loaded mostly with the Blackfoot annuities. Instead
of meeting the Robert Campbell, which we thought
would be the first boat up, we met Mr. Chouteau, on
the steamer Nellie Rogers, bound for Fort Benton.
This was at Fort Kipp, where we got on board to return to Fort Galpin, as we had learned that the Robert Campbell was yet far below. About 50 miles below Fort Galpin we met the Shreveport, on her return
from Benton. We boarded her and proceeded on
our way down; but she was to turn back to assist the
Robert Campbell up with the annuities. At Heart
river we met the Robert Campbell, and, as agreed
upon, we turned back in her company.

The third day afterward we were fired upon by a
party of Sioux, while wooding, but no one was hurt.
We went on again to a place called the Tobacco [13] Garden, about 100 miles below the mouth of the Yellowstone, where we saw a large war party of Sioux on the
south side of the river. The two boats came within
100 yards of each other, and anchored in the middle
of the river to see what those Indians were going to
do. After the Sioux had all gathered up, they cried
out for the boat, saying they wanted to have a talk,

[13] For this place, where the bloody affair about to be narrated
comes off, see note [13], p. 126. The distance I there give, 75 m.
below the Yellowstone by the channel of the Missouri, is a misprint for 95.

and were out of tobacco. There were two Indian agents on board, Major Latta for the Gros Ventres, Mandans, and Assiniboines, and Major Reed [14] for the Blackfeet. I was at the time on the Shreveport. The captain and those gentlemen, not knowing much about Indians, thought best to send for the head men of the party, and in spite of all that could be done from our boat to make them abandon the idea, Captain Joseph La Barge would send out the yawl. The first crew ordered refused to go; the mate, not wishing to insist on sending another crew, without further orders, reported to the captain that the men had refused, and was sent back very roughly with orders to send another crew. So seven men were ordered out. One young man of this crew, already in the yawl, caught hold of the steamboat, saying, " I don't want to go—we'll all be killed." The mate threatened to break his fingers if he did not loosen his hold, and he was obliged to go with the crew—never to return. As soon as they started I took my doublebarreled gun and ran up on the hurricane deck. When the Indians saw the yawl coming they jumped down the bank, and the moment the yawl landed, dis-

[14] Henry W. Reed of Iowa, a nondescript. He was Elder Reed at home, Major Reed abroad, and figures beyond as member of a certain Peace Commission for which Larpenteur was interpreter.

charged a volley, killing three men and wounding another, who, it was thought, would not recover.
From the steamboat we fired several volleys, but to
no effect. A few shots were afterward fired from the
willows by the Indians, also without effect, and about
three o'clock in the afternoon we got under way.[15]

[15] Boller, who was on the Robert Campbell, devotes his chap.
xxxv, pp. 363–369, to a more circumstantial account of this affair,
which I will give in substance. The Campbell, Capt. Joseph
La Barge, had on board Jerry Millington, the clerk; one McKin-
ney, pilot; the two Indian agents, Latta and Reed, whom Larpenteur names; Alexander Culbertson and his Blackfoot wife;
and a number of mountaineers and adventurers, the latter bound
for the newly discovered gold fields of Montana. At Fort Pierre
Mr. Charles reported the Indians to be very bad above. The
agents had a talk, through the interpreter, François La Fram-
boise, with some Sioux who were camped at Pierre, complaining
of the killing of eight Indians at Fort Randall a short time
before. At Heart River island the Campbell's rudder broke, and
while she was repairing, the Shreveport, which had discharged at
Cow island and hurried down to meet her, hove in sight. Car-
goes being rearranged, the two boats went up in convoy. When
at the mouth of L'Eau qui Mont, or Rising Water creek, the
Shreveport, in advance, stopped at a sandbar to take on drift-
wood. While she was thus occupied, several Indians appeared
on the opposite bank, and called out in Grosventre language for
a boat; they were returning from a hunt, had made plenty of meat,
and wished to trade for coffee and sugar. After this their horses
were turned out on the prairie to feed, the squaws were crossing
with the plunder in a bull boat, and the Campbell had just
tapped the signal-bell to start, when the Indian women gave a
piercing shriek. A Sioux on a white horse dashed out of a ravine.
making for the horses, and was followed by 15 or 20 others, who

The next day, at 10 a. m., we buried the three poor
fellows in one grave; the young man Martin was one
of them.   Two days afterward we reached the mouth

drove off the herd and disappeared. The Grosventres, who had
thus lost nearly all they possessed at one fell swoop, were taken
aboard the Campbell, provided for, and landed on the opposite
side, to make their way to the village.

The Campbell continued, and on rounding the point below
Shell creek sighted the Shreveport wooding. There was a commotion on the latter boat, which backed out into the channel and
made for the other shore. The Campbell followed, and the two
boats made fast together at a sand bar, as Larpenteur relates. It
was then learned on the Campbell that when the Shreveport had
stopped to wood, the hunter Dauphin went out as usual to look
for game, but discovered instead a large party of Sioux making for
the boat. He hurried back to give the alarm, the hawser was cut,
and the boat backed into the stream, as just said. That afternoon
was occupied in making a breastwork of flour sacks on the boiler
decks of both boats, in expectation of attack at any point they
might stop for wood. Soon after sunrise next morning a shot
was fired while the boats were running close into shore; the ball
passed through the pilot-house, narrowly missing one Atkins,
who was at the wheel of the Campbell. Mrs. Culbertson's sharp
eye soon afterward descried some distant objects, which proved
to be a party of Sioux, about 200 in number, moving in a direction to intercept the boats. The Shreveport, which was ahead,
dropped down, and both boats were made fast to a sand bar not
far from Tobacco Garden creek, while the Indians gathered on
the bank, protected and partly concealed in the woods. There
was no discipline on the Campbell, and no one seemed to know
what to do. The Indians yelled to the whites to come ashore
and be killed; that they wanted arms, ammunition, and provisions; that the whites were dogs, only fit to be killed—with
other demands, taunts, and threats to like effect. Several per-

of the Yellowstone, where both boats stopped, it being impossible for them to proceed farther.
Although they were on bad terms with the Ameri-

sons on board besides Mrs. Culbertson understood Sioux, and
there was no possible doubt of the Indians' meaning. Somebody
suggested to send a boat ashore to bring some of the leading men
aboard for a talk; and as neither of the Indian agents, Latta and
Reed, seemed to have any ideas of their own to advance, this
senseless suggestion was acted on. The Indians were meanwhile
gathered on the bank, insulting and defying the whites continually. The passengers were behind their breastworks of flour
sacks; among them were Jerry Millington, who had been a
trader on the Platte; Louis Elle, Boller himself, and several
others, close together; Culbertson and his wife stood near by.
To their unspeakable surprise a boat put off from the steamer
and headed for the shore. The agent, who might have em-
braced this opportunity to edify his red children in a talk, did
not go. As the boat left, Mrs. Culbertson called out to the crew,
"Come back! Come back! You'll all be killed!" But the men
bent to their oars, and neared the fatal shore. As the boat
landed, Indians crowded ominously upon her, and Millington remarked, "There'll be hell raised now." The Sioux chief sprang
into the yawl, and shook hands with each of the crew; a score of
dusky warriors were at his heels. Presently those on the steamer
saw weapons gleaming, white smoke puffing, and heard sharp
reports that told of slaughtered men. The fire was answered
from both boats, not without effect, as was seen by the hurried
movements of the Indians. The yawl with its load of dead and
wounded was soon floating down stream; one man was seen
clinging to her stern. Another boat was sent for her, and the
victims of this senseless affair were brought aboard. Two only
of the crew escaped; one of these, who had been wounded,
feigned death; the other was the steersman, who had the presence of mind to throw himself overboard, and cling to the boat

can Fur Company they concluded to ask Mr. Hodgkiss,[16] who was in charge, to let them store their goods
in Fort Union. Knowing that Mr. Hodgkiss was
very fond of liquor, they made sure of success, and
certainly succeeded.

When we came to the fort we learned that Malcolm
Clark had shot Owen McKenzie. Mr. Chouteau had
not been able to ascend the Missouri farther than
Milk river, where he had to put out all his freight, to

till he was rescued. So reluctant had these men been to start
that the mate [named Miller], drove them into the yawl with an
ax; he was afterward killed in a street brawl in Cincinnati. The
wounded man recovered. Next day the dead were decently
buried on the river bank, and stones piled over their graves to
keep the wolves from digging them up. Thus was avenged the
massacre of eight Indians at Fort Randall.

I have offered in writing to Captain Joseph La Barge to print
in this connection any statement concerning the affair that he
might wish to make and would be willing to sign; but up to date
of going to press have not heard from him. Where the blame,
if any, should rest, is to me a matter of entire indifference.

[16] " Mr. Hodgkiss of the American Fur Company entertained
me with interesting reminiscences of his life," says Boller, p. 263,
when he was at the Arickaras; "he being one of the veteran
mountaineers, having come up in 1832 as clerk for Captain
Bonneville." Again, p. 369, on the occasion when Boller was
still with Larpenteur: " Mr. Hodgkiss (formerly in charge of
Fort Clark) was now in command of this Post [Union], and in the
kindest manner tendered all the hospitality and assistance in his
power to those passengers who were disappointed in getting to
Fort Benton by steamer." This was in 1863. His death is given
beyond. Larpenteur copy spells his name Hudykits.

be hauled up to Benton with wagons.   While he was there McKenzie came down to the boat.   McKenzie had disputed with Clark in regard to some settlements of the time of Frost, Todd, and Co.   Clark had been in charge for that company, and McKenzie was not on good terms with him.   So McKenzie got very drunk and commenced to quarrel with Clark, who, knowing him to be a dangerous man, took out his pistol and shot three balls through McKenzie, killing him instantly.[17]   This one of Captain La Barge's best kind of men gone, there was no one in charge of Fort Galpin.   They put in charge Louis Dauphin, whom I

[17] Miss Helen P. Clarke's version of her father's part in this tragedy is as follows, Cont. Mont. Hist. Soc. ii, 1896, pp. 257–58: "It would be somewhat singular if a man with as strong characteristics as Malcolm Clarke should pass through life without making enemies.   To one it proved fatally disastrous—a man named [Owen] McKenzie.   Perhaps the less said of him the better.   The origin of the quarrel, a mere nothing.   Both were probably to blame.   Matters might have been amicably settled, but poor McKenzie's anger was fed and encouraged by his friends, and whiskey only added fuel to the flame.   At any rate, one summer in 1862 or 1863, at Fort Union, or near there, on the American Fur Company's boat, McKenzie, blinded with anger and drink, entered the cabin where my father was, and when within two feet of him levelled his pistol.   It is needless to say that the fatal charge was quickly turned, and McKenzie fell its victim.   And there he lay pulseless and cold with a bullet in his heart, calmer by far than the man that shot him, although the latter knew it was done in self defense, and was afterwards fully exonerated."

knew to be a regular thief, and who did not know his a b c of the business. Finding themselves in a bad fix about Galpin, they had the brass to ask me how I would like to go there again; but I bade them to be so kind as to excuse me, as they could find plenty of better men than myself. Shortly after this Dauphin was killed by the Sioux. A young man named Antoine Primeau was shot by Jerry Potts, a half-breed. My cook, a nice young man, who wanted to display his bravery, was killed by some Sioux near the fort. James Windle [Wendall?] was killed by a bull-driver who came down from Benton. All this happened at Fort Galpin shortly after I left, and the goods which the La Barges had brought up were nearly all lost.

The annuities being all stored, we started for the States. A few miles below Sioux City the mate had a quarrel with his hands, in which he stabbed one of them, who died in fifteen minutes. The gentlemanly La Barges, having treated all their clerks about the same as they did me, drew out of the Indian trade. This was in 1863.

CHAPTER XVIII.

(1864-66.)

IN the spring of 1864 I made arrangements with Mr. Charles Chouteau to take charge of Fort Union. As he was not ready to leave St. Louis, I started ahead of him on the steamer Benton, in charge of 50 tons of commissary freight, having been appointed as commissary by General Alfred Sully of the U. S. army. I was to be relieved on the arrival of his fleet, which was to be up during the summer. The main reason of my appointment was that we had 17 barrels of whiskey in this freight.

We left St. Louis on the 26th of March. On arriving at Fort Randall,[1] we learned that 1,500 lodges

[1] This military post was established by General Wm. S. Harney in 1856, and named for Surgeon B. Randall, U. S. A. A part of the material was brought from Fort Lookout in 1857. Randall stood on the right bank of the Missouri, ¼–½ m. from the water, and 50 feet above it, lat. 98° 34′ N., long. 34° 12′ W. The landing was at the 978¾-mile point of some charts. A little creek which made down alongside the fort became known as Garden creek, first

of Sioux were camped near Fort Berthold, determined to stop all navigation, and so placed that they
could sink boats by rolling rocks down the bank.
Those who knew neither the country nor the Indians
believed all this rubbish, and some of the ladies who
were on board, bound for Montana, expressed a de-
sire to turn back.   We kept on our voyage, which
was very tedious, on account of low water.

noticed by Lewis and Clark as they passed by Sept. 8, 1804 : see
L. and C., ed. 1893, p. 112. Across the river is a place called Swan,
or White Swan, Charles Mix Co., S. Dak.   The situation is 55 m.
in an air-line above Yankton—further by road, 26 m. further by
river.   Randall was not a bad sort of a place, for a military post.
I have pleasant memories of wintering there, 1872-73, though I
was not very well housed, did not fare sumptuously at table, and
sometimes had to go to bed to keep warm.   The post was almost
buried under the snow after a blizzard we had in April, when
some of the drifts were level with the roofs.   I made large
collections in natural history that season, and wrote my Field
Ornithology, which appeared in 1874.   The best poker-player I
ever faced—for I never happened to play with General Custer—
was Capt. John Hartley of the 22d Infantry—a good soldier who
got into trouble, resigned Sept. 7, 1882, and blew out his brains
in a shooting gallery in New York City, Mar. 10, 1883, because
he had not money enough to buy any means of self-destruction,
and could get a shot at himself without paying for it first.   He
was a nervy fellow, of very ready wit, whom I always liked.
The Benton, on which Larpenteur reached Randall, was a stern-
wheeler of 246 tons, owned by Durfee and Peck ; Capt. Frank
Dozier, master, May 19, 1869, when she was snagged 8 m. above
De Soto, Washington Co., Neb., giving name to Benton Bend of
the Missouri.

On the 6th of May we reached Fort Sully[2] with a part of our load, having been obliged to make a double trip. On our arrival Colonel Bartlett, in command of Sully, informed us that, owing to reports of hostile Indians being strongly forted near Berthold, he had just received a dispatch from headquarters, ordering him to prevent any steamers from going farther up till a sufficient number arrived to justify him in sending an escort with them, which was left, in a great measure, to his own judgment. He said that he would let us know shortly what he would determine upon, and requested the captain to call again

[2] *Old* Fort Sully, below Fort Pierre—not the other one of the same name, which was later built above Pierre : see Lewis and Clark, pp. 131 and 146. The old fort stood on the left (N.) bank of the Missouri, opposite the head of Farm island, above the Padani Tiyohe or Pawnees Deserted river, and 4½ m. below Pierre, S. Dak., by the C. and N. W. R. R., which now runs through the site. This post was built by order of General Sully in the fall of 1863, but abandoned because the situation proved insalubrious. Larpenteur notes, in his Orig. Journ. at date of Aug. 1, 1866, that the Fort had been abandoned and the soldiers had gone up river to build another. New Fort Sully was begun July 25, 1866, 30 m. higher up river on the same side, 18 or 20 m. below Cheyenne river, lat. 44° 35′ N., long. 100° 36′ W., alt. 2,000 feet; completed in 1868. It stood on the third rise from the river, about 160 feet above the water, and about the same below the highest ground in the rear. The reservation in which it was situated included 27,000 acres. A detailed description, by Surgeons Gray and Wright, U. S. A., occupies pp. 388-390 of Circular No. 4, Surgeon General's Office, Washington, 1870.

the next day. Being anxious to move on, and not
putting much faith in any such stories as we had
learned, we called on the commander. As I was a
commissary, and had been for many years with the
Indians, he would have me let him know what I
thought about the matter. To which I replied that
I thought all those reports, like many others, much
exaggerated, and should not be at all surprised if we
did not see a single Indian on our journey. For one
thing there was no game on the river, and it was impossible for 1,500 lodges to remain long in camp together; and as to any place where they could roll
rocks down the bank and sink the boat, I knew of
none such—at which he smiled. As to danger, I
could not say there was none; we might be fired on
and some persons might be killed, but as there were
nearly 150 men on board, all well armed, I did not
apprehend   much   danger.   The   greatest   danger
would be at night, but good care would be taken to
always anchor on a sand bar in the middle of the
river.   Colonel Bartlett then asked the captain when
he thought he would be ready to leave; the answer
was, "In a couple of days."   "Well," said he, "when
you are ready, let me know; something more favorable may turn up in that time."

With the consent of the commander we resumed
our journey on the 9th of May. The river being still

very low, we made but slow progress.[3] No Indians
were seen until we came to the mouth of Heart river,
where, on the 24th, about 9 a. m. we discovered a few
Indians in the broken banks of the Missouri, awaiting
our arrival with the American flag hoisted. Being
well prepared, we landed, and gave them some few
provisions and a little tobacco. They were but 12 in
all—a half-starved looking set. After proceeding
about 10 miles, we saw three Indians, who desired us
to land; we did so, and found that one of them was
Black Catfish, chief of the Yanctonais, who showed
his papers from General William S. Harney. Having given them a good cup of coffee on board, and a
few presents, we again got under way; and those
were the last Indians we saw.

We landed safe and sound at Union on the last day

[3] During which occurred an incident which the Autobiog. does
not give. I find in an Orig. Journ., p. 13, at date of Sunday, May
8, 1864, the following : " The weather very fine but the times
rather boisterous on board the mate having quite a row with one
of his hands by whom the mate went near loosing his nose by a
bite. It was all stoped without much farther injury, the biting
individual and his comrade were discharged and left at this
place."

Larpenteur's Orig. Journ. of this trip, and other diaries, in-
complete, 1864-72, are now in my hands, having lately been sent
to me by his widow, at the instance of my friend Mr. Mitchell
Vincent. They are thus available for checking the main text of
the rest of his narrative, as well as for furnishing some additional
notes.

of May, being the first boat up this season.   We arrived early in the morning and came in sight of the
fort unobserved.   The doors were all closed, and not
a living object was stirring except some buffalo, pas-
turing about 300 yards from the fort.   But the door
was soon opened, the flag hoisted, and the artillery
fired; to which salute the boat responded.   We were
informed that the Sioux had been, and were still, so
bad that the men dared not keep the doors open.
The Indians had at one time made a rush, and shot
a squaw through the thigh just as she was entering the
fort.   The Benton left about 3 p. m., having discharged 50 tons of freight, which pleased the passengers very much.

I have omitted to say that, while at Berthold, I was
informed of Mr. Hodgkiss' death; this news had not
reached St. Louis when I left.   Mr. I. C. Rolette was
then in charge.

I was not to take charge of Union until the return
of Mr. Chouteau from Benton.   On the 13th of June
Mr. Chouteau arrived with his steamer, the Yellowstone, bringing a company of soldiers for the protection of the fort, and of the Assiniboines; it was
Company I, Wisconsin Volunteers, commanded by
Captain Greer, and Major Wilkinson, the Indian
agent, also arrived.   The Yellowstone left for Benton the same day.

On the 2d day of July the Yellowstone returned
from Benton, and, after all arrangements had been
made, I took charge of Fort Union for the last year
of the American Fur Company; but I still retained
my position as commissary until the arrival of General Sully's fleet.

Now a few words[4] in regard to that expedition.
Previous to my leaving St. Louis General Sully, one
day, while at Mr. Chouteau's office, took pains to tell
me the route he was going to take to the mouth of
the Bighorn.   He showed me the map, observing
that the route from Heart river, at which point he intended to leave the Missouri and strike for the Horn,
was the shortest, and could be accomplished in little
time.   I had been on the Horn, and had also traveled
some on the Little Missouri.   I knew the latter to be
very rough country, which, further up than I had
been, was almost all Bad Lands.   This made me observe that I thought he would have a great deal of

[4] " A few words " more than Larpenteur gives on the subject
may be read in two papers in the Contributions to the Historical
Society of Montana, vol. ii, 1896.   One of these, entitled General
Alfred Sully's Expedition of 1864 . . . from the diary of Judge
Nicholas Hilger, pp. 314–328, is subtitled Battle with the Com-
bined Tribes of Sioux Indians among the Bad Lands of the
Little Missouri.   The other, headed General Sully's Expedition
of 1864 Against the Sioux, by Nathaniel Pope, occupies pp. 329,
330.   Both are of course aside from the official military report.

trouble in getting through with his command; but
with a map and some good brandy, in Chouteau's
office, one can get through anywhere. I found him
convinced that he would meet with little difficulty;
but I was satisfied to the contrary. After this he
went on with his talk, saying, " I have a fleet of five
steamers, which are going up as far as Union.
Among them I have two light ones, intended to bring
up all the goods and implements to the mouth of the
Horn, where I expect to meet them. This notion I
knew would never be realized; he might get to the
Horn with his command, but for a steamboat to ascend the Yellowstone that distance I knew to be impossible,⁵ and was much surprised at the idea.

Now we will return to Fort Union, and relate what
took place until the arrival of the fleet.⁶   Captain

⁵ It is said that the improbable always happens, and it is quite
true that what is supposed to be the impossible sometimes does.
During the Sioux war of 1876, which culminated on June 25 in
the Custer massacre, a steamer was not only up the Yellowstone
to the Bighorn, but up the latter to the Little Bighorn, June 29.
" The Far West was waiting for us at the mouth of the Little
Big Horn. . . The Far West left that day for the mouth of the
Big Horn," says General Gibbon, Rep. Secy. of War, i, 1876, p.
474. Larpenteur never heard of such light-draft boats as were
built after his time, and perhaps lacked the sagacity attributed
to a celebrated scientist who is reported to have said that no one
should use the word "impossible" outside of mathematics.

⁶ Tues., July 19, 1864. "Pierre Chêne, Bellehumeur, and young
Van Court arrived on horseback from Ft. Benton reported that

Greer had not been long stationed in the fort when a war party of Sioux, early one morning, stole all the horses, not more than 40 steps from one of the bastions. He started a detail of 20 men in pursuit on foot; had the Indians been so disposed, they could have destroyed those men with all ease. Two weeks later another party made an attack.[7] It happened that there were a few Gros Ventres of the Missouri at the fort, who, with some soldiers, succeeded in overtaking one of the Sioux; they pretty soon returned with his scalp, ears, and nose, and a great scalp dance followed. After this everything went

the Sioux had killed three men at Fort Galpin and wounded another and many cattle. The fort is now abandoned." Orig. Journ., p. 46.

[7] The exact date is Friday, July 29, 1864. " Early this morning at about 5 o'clock an alarm of Indians was cried, very shortly a discharge of guns was heard, and the Sioux were seen going off with two horses taken from an Assiniboine party which arrived last night—Redstone, chief of sixty lodges of the band of Canoes. These Indians, some Grosventres, who came from below in the expedition boats, and some soldiers started in pursuit and overtook the enemy; killed one and brought in his scalp, one hand and one foot, saying that they had killed more, but could not get them. Two Assiniboines were wounded, one through the thigh and left arm, breaking no bones, the other with an arrow in his stern. None of the soldiers was wounded, but the Indians acknowledged that had it not been for the soldiers' arrival so soon, the Sioux might have killed them all. The Assiniboines were but four, the Sioux seventeen. They got back their horses, and killed one Sioux," Orig. Journ., p. 51.

smoothly[8] till the 20th of November [1864], when a party of 83 miners arrived on their return trip to the States by the Yellowstone; they had been frozen in about 20 miles from the mouth of that river, and obliged to abandon their boats. Finding that they could not all be entertained comfortably in the fort, and some wishing to go to the States, half of the party made up their minds to take it afoot. Those remaining would have proved very troublesome, and more dangerous than the hostile or friendly Indians, had not Captain Greer, who was quartered in the fort, kept them quite civil. They were a rough set. Early in the spring [1865] I made them a large Mackinaw, in which they left two days after the ice broke, on the 17th of April. Captain Greer went with them, to meet the steamer Yellowstone.

We were not troubled by the hostiles that winter [1864-65], and should have had a pleasant time, had

[8] Sunday, Aug. 7, 1864. "Early this morning a party of 22 miners arrived from Virginia City by way of the Yellowstone in two small boats which they made up the Bighorn. They left Virginia City on the 22d [of July]. They report that there is no gold on the head of the Yellowstone, but that the Virginia mines are good. They saw the steamers [Chippewa Falls and Alone] yesterday morning about 20 miles below Brazeau's houses; and report that 60 wagons had just arrived at the mouth of the Big horn," Orig. Journ., p. 56. It thus appears that the party of miners of Nov. 20 was not the first such to reach Union in 1864.

not scurvy broken out toward the end of that season; three soldiers died.   As we had seen no enemies all winter, when spring came the soldiers went
out hunting in all directions, as though there was no
danger, and became very careless.   On the 26th of
April [1865] two of them returned from a hunt, and
said they had found the remains of an elk which had
been wounded and died, and was partly eaten up by a
grizzly bear.   The orderly sergeant and those two men
agreed to go early next morning° to see if they could
get a shot at Mr. Grizzly, and gave orders to the
guard to awake them by daylight.   The guard did as
he had been ordered, and the three hunters went after
the bear.   When they had gone about three-quar-
ters of a mile, and were passing through some thick
bushes, they were fired upon by a party of concealed

° Thurs., Apr. 27, 1865, in substance as follows : About six
o'clock the orderly and two soldiers were attacked by Sioux in
going down in the point to hunt a bear.   The orderly was killed
on the spot; he had eleven wounds, all with arrows; was scalped
and entirely stripped of clothing.   One of the soldiers was shot
in the right side above the heart, and had two shots in the left
thigh and one in the right, all with balls ; the doctor said he
might recover, but it was doubtful.   The third soldier killed an
Indian, whom they scalped; and from signs they discovered were
pretty certain they had killed three altogether.   The Sioux were
about 25 in number.

Apr. 28.   At 3 p. m. buried the orderly, and about five a file of
soldiers went and hung up the body of the dead Sioux.—Orig.
Journ., pp. 123, 124.

hostiles, about 40 in number, and one of them was shot down. Another of them shot and killed an Indian. The orderly sergeant, who had had the scurvy, could not run; the Indians rushed upon him, shot nine arrows into him, pounded him with their war-clubs, and then scalped him, not leaving a hair upon his head. The young man who fell at the first discharge was shot with one ball, above his left breast, and two in his leg. The bushes were thick where he was lying, and he saw them looking for him; but as the alarm had been given at the fort, by the guard, who had seen and heard the firing, they had no time to search, and ran away, leaving their own dead man. In the afternoon a party of soldiers went to the spot and hung him in some elm trees where he could be seen dangling from the Fort.[10]

Nothing worthy of note took place from this time till the arrival of the Yellowstone, on the 5th of June. Mr. Chouteau arrived this time in great distress; having been reported as a rebel he could not obtain a license, and was obliged to sell out all his trading-posts, except Benton; all other posts he sold to Hubble, Hawley and Co., of which A. B. Smith of Chicago was the head; it was called the North West Fur Company.[11] This being the case, we immediately set to

[10] " The corpse was still dangling from the elm tree when I arrived at the fort in 1865," writes Dr. Matthews to me, 1897.

[11] Wed., July 5, 1865, the Orig. Journ. notes that the steamer

work taking the inventory. When the post was turned over to the N. W. Co. I made arrangements to take charge of it for this new firm. Captain Upton of the regulars,[12] who arrived to relieve Captain Greer, had instructions to take possession of Fort Union for the United States, and turn all citizens out. So I had to turn out my men, and would have been obliged to leave myself, had not the captain suffered me to keep my own room and my cook. I thus found myself, as it were, under arrest, but this did not last long.[13]

Hattie May returned to Union, having gone 12 m. above Milk river, where they made a fort to store their goods, called Fort Kaiser or Keiser, near Fort Copelin, which was built for the same purpose. Little has ever been heard of either of these two posts, which must have been in close vicinity of Fort Galpin.

[12] Larpenteur is mistaken here—this officer was not Emory Upton, Capt. 5th U. S. Artillery Feb. 22, 1865, and the only one of that name in the regular army, but a Capt. Upton of Co. B of the 1st U. S. Vols.—one of those regiments which used to be called "galvanized rebels," composed of rebel prisoners released on condition that they would fight Indians for us. I have failed to find the date of Capt. Upton's arrival. The name reminds me to say that a certain official map marks "Old Fort Upton" in the position of Union. I once suspected that some temporary post bore that name, but am now satisfied "Upton" is merely a misprint for Union.

[13] "Captain Upton left with most of his company on the 14th. Lieut. Young and a few men remained a few days, to sell goods and pack up. I was with them," Dr. Matthews, in *lit*. The Orig. Journ. is still more explicit : Sunday, Aug. 13. Express arr. at Union from Berthold with Gen. Sully's orders to Co. B.

On the 14th of August Captain Upton was ordered
away, and I was again in full possession of the fort.
Two days afterward Mr. Frederick D. Pease,[14] a member of the Company, arrived to attend the sale of the
commissary goods. He asked my opinion in regard
to sending after the Crows, who, he thought, had still
many robes. I remarked that I would not send; that
they could not have much left to trade, as so many
boats had been up the river; and, for another thing.

Lieut. Young and 20 soldiers will remain until the steamer
returns, but there will be no soldiers left during the winter.

14th. Capt. Upton left at 1.30 p. m. with about 80 men; the lieutenant and doctor [Young and Matthews] remained with 18 men.

[14] The same for whom Fort F. D. Pease was named. This was
built early in 1875 by a party of about 40 men from Bozeman,
Mont., under Mr. Pease. The situation was on the N. (left) bank
of the Yellowstone, at or near present Etchetah, Custer Co., between Allen's coulée and Alkali creek. The low land along here
became known as Pease's bottom ; and the next stream below
Alkali creek bears the alternative names of Pease's and Van
Horn's creek (Windsor's creek of Lewis and Clark, ed. 1893, p.
1156), which falls into the Yellowstone nearly opposite Myers.
Fort Pease was primarily a trading post, but the design was to
colonize and lay out a town in this favorable situation. Then
came the Sioux war; the fort was continually beleaguered, and
skirmishing was incessant ; many Indians were killed, but not
without loss of six of the garrison dead and still more wounded.
The whites were reduced to 28, appealed to the military for assistance, and on Feb. 22, 1876, Major James S. Brisbin left Fort Ellis
with four companies of the 2d Cavalry for the relief of Fort
Pease. The post was abandoned in March, but found convenient
to use as a storehouse when, on April 21, it was temporarily

that I knew Captain Greer, during the past winter, had created such a jealousy between them and the Assiniboines that if they met it was sure to be war. So I did not think advisable to send; it would be better to wait till the arrival of the agent.   But, in spite of all I said or could do, he would send.   After the sale he left, and I remained with six men in a place where a company of soldiers had once been thought required for safety.

On the 21st [15] of August Mr. Pease and all the Gov-

occupied by troops under Gibbon's command in the Sioux campaign.   See Lt. Bradley's account of these movements in Cont. Mont. Hist. Soc. ii, 1896, pp. 174, 175.   But it appears *ibid.*, p. 137, from what my friend Peter Koch of Bozeman says, that the citizens took a somewhat different view of the situation.   "The names of Crook and Gibbon and Miles will always be household words in Montana.   But when Gen. Brisbin seems to believe the little garrison at Fort Pease was listening for his bugles, as the garrison at Lucknow listened for the pipes of Havelock, he was never more mistaken in his life.   That garrison was ready to hold the fort much longer, and if not forced by Gen. Brisbin's orders to leave, Fort Pease would never have been surrendered."   We may judge the facts to have been, that the garrison needed the relief ; and that, having received it, they did not wish to leave.

[16] It appears from entries in the Orig. Journ. that all government affairs at Union ended with the sale of commissary stores to Smith, Hubble, Hawley and Co. at noon of Monday, Aug. 21, 1865, and when the steamer Big Horn left, at 5 p. m. that day, Larpenteur remained in charge with Mr. Herrick as clerk, six working men, and the individual whom the Journ. variously styles Charles Kuncle, Cunkle, Kunland, or Konkland.   Dr. Matthews,

ernment officers left Fort Union; I resumed full
charge, being left with six working men, one clerk,
and one loafer named Conklin, who Mr. Pease said
he thought was a Government spy, and who turned
out to be a perfect blatherskite. After the departure
of all the force which had been stationed here the
men at times became quite unruly, and threatened to

who knew him, gives me the right name of this amusing swindler,
and tells the following good story:

"Conklin was a tall, muscular man, apparently between 30 and
40 years of age in 1865. He always spoke of himself as 'Captain'
Conklin; but my opinion is that he signed his own commission.
He said he had been a captain of scouts under Gen. Sully in 1864;
this is doubtful, but if he was, the title was only complimentary.
He allowed it to be inferred that he was in the secret service, and
pretended to be high in influence with the powers that be—President and Secretary of War included. According to his own
account he had had no end of thrilling adventures and hair-
breadth escapes during the war and at other times. He was
a blatant Hibernian who, if you would believe him, you
would think knew everything and everybody, and had been
everywhere. He was plausible and imposed on many shrewd
people for awhile. When the troops abandoned Fort Union, in
1865, Conklin remained behind without salary; but drawing his
rations. The traders were willing to have another man in their
weak garrison, and thus our author came, in time, to know his
character.

"While our troops were still at Fort Union, he was employed
by a steamboat captain, working for an opposition company, to
carry a message to a new trading station somewhere about the
mouth of Milk river, and was to get $100 for his ride. He mounted
a horse, lay out in the prairie for a week, until he got well sun-
burnt, and then came back, saying that the Crows (a friendly

leave, which made it very disagreeable to me. During the night of September 10th the forerunners of the Crows arrived, with three white men who had been in their camps, reporting that these Indians would be in next day. There happened to be in the Fort a few young Assiniboines, who left that same night for their camp, about 20 miles distant. In the

tribe) had taken him prisoner and would not let him go through. It was too late in the season to send another messenger, for the steamer, owing to low water, was obliged to return to St. Louis. The plans of the opposition miscarried. He got his $100; but we all suspected that he got another $100 from the agent of the Northwest Fur Co. *not* to go through. [It appears from Orig. Journ. that "Konkland" started for Fort Copelin on express Aug. 24 and returned on the 30th, having been taken prisoner, as he affirmed, by Crows, who carried him to their camp, recognizing the mare he rode and thinking he had stolen her, etc.]

"After I left him at Fort Union I heard the following tale: Once he was traveling, with troops, in an ambulance or wagon, sitting beside the driver, and insisted on taking the reins. 'Can you drive a six-mule team?' said the doubting driver. 'To be sure! I've dhruv twinty mules through the Rocky Mounthins,' he answered. The driver surrendered the reins to him, and soon they came to a gully where Conklin mismanaged the team, upset the wagon, broke the tongue, and nearly killed himself and the driver. 'What did you tell me you'd driven twenty mules through the mountains for? You don't know how to drive one,' roared the driver, with many a choice oath. Conklin pulled himself out of the ruins, pale as a ghost, and, when he got breath, answered: ' Faix, I dhruv ivery wan of thim; but sure they were all *loose*.'

"I heard many more such traditions of him afterward; but this will suffice to paint his character."

mean time the Crows arrived, with but little to trade, and camped close to the fort—about 200 in all, men and women. On their arrival the chief demanded the annuities, but, as I had not been instructed to give them, I declined, but promised that if the agent did not arrive within eight days, I would then do as he desired. He said that was a long time, but finally agreed to wait; but trade commenced, and all went on well.

On the 12th of September, 1865,[16] a little before sunrise, I was awakened by my interpreter, saying, " Mr. Larpenteur—the Sioux! the Sioux! they have made a rush on the Crow horses, driven them all off, and are now fighting." I immediately got up, and ran up on the gallery; by this time the Indians had got out of sight, but I could hear the firing. A little while afterward the report came that there were some Assiniboines among them. By another dispatch we learned that they were all Assiniboines, that the

[16] " Tues. Sept. 12, 1865. Great excitement ! About sunrise the cry of 'Sioux !' was heard ; in a very little time the Crows were engaged in a fight, and very soon we learned that it was the Assiniboines, of which they killed four, and one Sioux. There were very few Sioux among them. The Assiniboines succeeded in getting off 101 head of horses, but the Crows took 55 head from them. Three Crows were slightly wounded. The Crows behaved remarkably well; they would not dance the Assiniboines scalps, and gave them to us to bury." Orig. Journ. of that date, in substance.

Crows had already killed two, and were still fighting. After the battle we learned that there were four Assiniboines killed, two Crows wounded, not dangerously; and that the latter had lost 45 head of horses. It was fortunate for us that no Crows were killed; for, had there been, we could not have saved the Assiniboines who were in the fort at the time; and it was only after a great deal of talk that we pacified the Crows. Then the chief, called Rotten Tail, came to me and said, " You must give me the annuities. You see that we cannot remain here any longer, the Assiniboines will have some more of our horses if we do." The old chief was right; I could no longer refuse him his annuities, and granted his request. But a little while afterward he came in with his soldiers, requesting me to give him the Assiniboines' annuities in payment for the 45 horses they had stolen, and also saying that the Crows must have ammunition. I saw plainly that they meant no good. I told the old Chief that I would give him his annuities, but that I had nothing else to give him, and that if he wanted pay for his horses he would have to wait till his father arrived on the steamer, which I expected would be up in a few days. Seeing that something was wrong, I had my men all well armed, and the cannon loaded. After a little more argument on the subject, the old fellow concluded to take his annuities. I then took

him into the warehouse and showed him his pile, saying, " This is yours, just as it was sent up. Here are
your papers, calling for so many boxes, sacks, barrels, and bales. You can see that none of them have
been opened. Now I will send them out to your
camp. You can remain here, to see that they all go,
and after that you can divide them to suit yourselves."
He then remarked that he would rather have me divide
them. I told him I would have nothing more to do
with them; that Indians always accused the whites of
stealing annuities, which was my reason for refusing
to make any division. Then he asked if I would let
my " little whites," as the laboring men are called,
divide, or help divide. I told him that would be as
they chose. Finally the goods were divided, and the
next morning, when all were ready to leave, the old
chief came to me in the best of humor, saying, " Well,
I have come to take breakfast with you before I go,
and see if you have any more documents for me to
sign." I told him I had some breakfast for him to
eat, but no documents to be signed. When the old
man was ready to go he shook hands in a very
friendly manner, saying, " I am well pleased, but
sorry that my friends the Assiniboines have been
fools. You can tell them, from me, that I am still
their friend, and willing to smoke with them. The
scalps which were taken were given to your interpre-

ter to bury and were not allowed to be danced, as we do with those of our enemies." Upon which he put the whip to his horse, and it was good-by, Mr. Crow. This being the result of Mr. Pease's dispatch.

On the 17th of September the Hattie May arrived, bringing Mr. A. B. Smith,[17] the Chicago hypocrite,

[17] This was the younger Mr. Smith, son of the head of the firm of Hubble, Hawley & Co. I know nothing to speak of about the firm or their affairs, but have no doubt that the Hawley here in mention is the person who has given us several place-names. Fort Hawley was situated in the bottom under the bluffs on the S. side of the Missouri, just about 20 m. above the Musselshell. There is also Hawley island, in Hawley cut-off from Hawley bend; nearest place generally known is Wilder P. O., Fergus Co., Mont., where the Circle Bar Cattle Co. have their corral, etc., between 3 and 4 m. higher than where the fort stood. The cut-off, I believe, is comparatively recent; but the bend is very old, as Lewis and Clark sailed around it on May 22, 1805, when the little stream they called Grouse creek fell into its bight from the area known as Hawley basin, on the N. This is the one correctly marked Beauchamp creek on the latest Mo. R. Comm. chart, which letters Grouse creek on the next one above, by error. Of this I am sure, for I have the L. and C. courses, showing that they went around Hawley bend, and it was on one of these courses in the bend that they named Grouse creek: see ed. of 1893, p. 319, where I make the correct identification. The G. L. O. map is in error in affixing the name of Beauchamp to a creek still higher than either of the two foregoing. This is Teapot creek of L. and C., not passed by them till the 23d, a mile above their camp of the 22d; it is the one marked Kannuck creek on the Commission chart, and sometimes also called Yellow creek. All three of the streams here in question are small, consecutive, and on the same side of the Missouri.

Mr. Hawley, and Mr. Pease. Having found myself
slighted, and not liking the proceedings of this new
firm, I requested my discharge of Mr. Pease last
August; but he then said he could not do that, and I
would have to await the arrival of the steamer.   On
her arrival I was discharged.   The steamer on which
I went left at noon next day,[18] and was to wait for
those gentlemen in the point below Union, where
the captain would take on a little wood; but as they
did not come at the appointed time, he went down to
the Fort William landing, only 2½ miles by land,
to wait for them there.   While landed there I found
that I had forgotten some documents, which I had
left with Mr. Thomas Campbell,[19] and wanted to go
back to the fort for them.   A great many ponies were
seen, supposed to be those of Sioux, which had kept
those gentlemen at the fort.   But I knew that the
Assiniboines were camped near by and that the ponies

[18] Tuesday, Sept. 19, 1865. " Left early this morning, but did
not make more than 1½ mile before we got aground where we
lost three hours in getting off, and went and stoped for the night
at the tobacco garden," says Orig. Journ., p. 163.   The down
voyage was: Berthold, 21st; Rice, 24th; Sully, 30th; "met
steamer Calypso having on board four commissioners to make
peace with the Sioux or another abortion," Oct. 1; Randall, 2d ;
Sioux City, 4th, as text states at conclusion of this chapter; and
home on the Little Sioux next day.

[19] "Tom " Campbell was a well and widely known man in all
that country for many years.   He was no relative of the Robert

were those of this party, who, on hearing the cannon firing at the arrival of the boat, had come to the fort. Now that it was nearly dark, and those gentlemen had not arrived, the captain, who knew that I wanted to go to the fort, said, " Larpenteur, if you want to go you can; I will not leave to-night." I asked someone to accompany me, but none dared go, saying, " Those Indians may be Sioux "; so I started alone. The fort was locked up on my arrival, and, as my business was with Campbell, who was in a small cabin about 100 yards off, I passed by the fort. There I saw many of my old friends among the Assiniboines, who shook hands with me, saying they were sorry to see me go. Having been satisfied about the documents I started back to the boat. During my absence those gentlemen arrived in a skiff. Not knowing, as yet, that I had gone to the fort, they said that it was a good thing for me that I was not at the fort,

Campbell so often mentioned in earlier parts of Larpenteur's narrative. I have already mentioned the ruins of one of his posts, which I saw at Benton in 1893. On the 1st of July, 1874, the Northern Boundary Survey, of which I was surgeon and naturalist, was opposite another old trading establishment known as " Tom Campbell's houses," which stood on the right (S.) bank of Milk river, about long. 106° 53′ W., below the mouth of Little Rocky creek, and at or near present station Vandalia on the G. N. Ry. From this point the main party kept on, but Captain W. F. Gregory's, to which I was specially attached, turned off N. next day, en route via Ft. Turnay on Frenchman's creek to 49°.

for the Assiniboines would surely have killed me;
then blaming me for that scrape with the Crows.   At
this the captain remarked, " Larpenteur has just gone
to the fort."   " Well," said they, " it is not good for
him; we should not be surprised if he does not return."   Not long after that I fired off my pistol and
the yawl came for me.   When the captain told me
what had been said, I remarked that, if I had been
obliged to leave the country whenever Indians threatened to kill me, I should have been gone long ago.

We left next morning, and, without anything
worthy of notice, reached Sioux City on the 4th of
October.   Having remained at Little Sioux river a
week, I started for St. Louis, to have a settlement
with Mr. Chouteau.   He received me like a gentleman, being pleased with the winding up of his affairs
at Union.   We settled up satisfactorily to both parties, and then I returned to pass the winter at my
place.

CHAPTER XIX.

(1866-72.)

ON AND AFTER THE PEACE COMMISSION.

On the 29th of April, 1866, I received an appointment from Governor Edmond as interpreter with the Peace Commissioners for the Assiniboines. I started immediately for Yankton, went on to Randall by stage, and then by land to Sully, at which point I boarded the steamer Sunset, and reached Fort Union on the 11th of June.[1]

[1] Dates of this paragraph verified by ref. to Orig. Journ. "The journalist," as Larpenteur is fond of styling himself in these years, found his appointment on the Commission awaiting him at his home on Sunday, Apr. 29, when he returned from a short visit to Sioux City. He left the latter place May 12; was at Randall 17th, and Sully 22d, where he took the Sunset 24th. On June 1 the diary speaks of a place curiously called " La Coulée de la Bardache or Morprodite valley." This is the situation of La Grace P. O., Campbell Co., S. Dak., 4½ m. (direct) S. of the border of N. Dak., where Hermaphrodite creek flows into the left side of the Missouri. The stream is Spring creek of some maps, Bordache creek of Heap's, and Bourbeuse R. of Warren's; it is Pond creek of Gass' Journ., 1807, p. 54; and originally Stone Idol creek of L. and C., Oct. 13, 1805: see ed. of

On my arrival I found that the Assiniboines had
been sent for; they soon came in, and I had everything arranged for the treaty on the arrival of the
steamer Ben Johnson, on which the commissioners
were coming.[2] They were Governor Edmond of
Dakota Territory, General Curtis of Iowa, Judge
Gurnsey of Wisconsin, Elder W. Reed of anywhere,
and Mr. M. K. Armstrong, secretary. The treaty,
like many others which were never realized, was
made for the purchase of all the Assiniboine lands
on the south side of the Missouri, and 20 miles square
on the north side, directly opposite the mouth of the
Yellowstone river. In consideration of this they

1893, p. 165. Besides the myth which the explorers give, there
is some unwritten history about the name of this stream.

[2] The Ben Johnson was a large side-wheeler owned by a person
of that name in the St. Louis and Omaha trade, chartered by
Capt. Joseph La Barge for the commissioners' trip at $300 per
day. A few years afterward she was snagged somewhere
between Brownville and Nemaha City, Nemaha Co., Neb., raised,
and finally destroyed by fire at St. Louis. On the arrival of
this boat the affairs of the treaty continued till July 19, when
Larpenteur left on her with the Commission for St. Louis.

A Report of the Northwestern Treaty Commission, etc., being
Paper No. 64, pp. 168-176, of Ann. Rep. Comm. Ind. Aff., in
Mess. and Docs., Interior Dept., 1866-67, is signed by Newton
Edmunds, S. R. Curtis, Orrin Guernsey, and Henry W. Reed,
Commissioners. Armstrong's name does not appear in that
connection, but Moses K. Armstrong, b. Ohio, was secretary of
a Peace Commission to the Sioux. Major-General S. R. Curtis
of Iowa is well known. See also No. 112, p. 240.

were to receive $30,000 per annum, for the term of
20 years; and I, for my children, was to get a section
of land wherever I chose to take it on the Assiniboine land; but nothing of this was realized.

The following summer General Sully was sent by
the department to treat with the Assiniboines. At
the council they asked him if he knew anything of the
boat which was to fetch them money according to
last summer's treaty. He told them he knew nothing
about it. They said they thought it very singular, if
he came from their great father's house, that he knew
nothing about their boat. Then they told him he
lied like all the others; that they had been filled with
talk up to their throats, and did not want any more.
A few annuities were sent them this year, but, as bad
luck would have it, the steamer [3] on which the goods
were coming sunk, and their groceries were all lost.

General Sully's object was to find out something
about the treaty of last summer, and to show them
what could be done without an Indian's having
Ely Samuel Parker [4] as an example, and Father De

[3] Very likely the boat to which Larpenteur refers was the
Pocahontas No. 2, a side-wheeler 180 x 32 feet, which was engaged
in carrying Indian annuities when she was snagged at Pocahontas isl., Aug. 10, 1866.

[4] I have inserted the full name of this distinguished officer,
which Larpenteur does not give. He was a captain of New
York volunteers from May 25, 1863, to Aug. 30, 1864, when he

Smet to inspire them with a conviction that the truth was spoken. I will say nothing of what remarks the Indians made. General Sully's commission was the most useless one I ever saw in the country, and the great Peace Commission was a complete failure.

On the 19th of July we left Union. On reaching the landing at Buford we learned that the Sioux had fired on the traders whom Mr. Gaben had sent from Union to them, after obtaining permission of the Peace Commissioners to do so. One was shot in the back with an arrow; and at least one ball glanced off the other, having struck the brass mounting of his belt. The fort was set on fire last night; but as many were moving about, it was discovered in time, and no injury was done. Having stolen many goods the Indians made their escape. The boat took on all that was left, and we proceeded down river.

As the treaty had not been made coming up, the Commission had to stop at Berthold, which we reached on the 21st of July. The council was held

became General Grant's military secretary, serving a year in that capacity; after about another year as a subaltern in the 2d Cavalry, he was appointed a colonel on Grant's staff as aid-de-camp from July 25, 1866, to Mar. 4, 1869. He was brevetted brigadier general for gallant and meritorious services in the campaign which ended with Lee's surrender, and resigned Apr. 26, 1869. General Parker was a full-blooded Indian.

next day. As the interpreter, Pierre Garreau, could
not speak good English, I was appointed to interpret
from his French into English. As the Gros Ventres did not feel inclined to sell their lands—at least,
the portion the Commissioners wanted—the council
lasted a long while. In some of their speeches the
Commissioners remarked that they had treated with
all the neighboring tribes, who would all be well off,
and the Gros Ventres alone would remain poor; even
some of the Sioux, who were considered hostile,
had made peace, and now would listen to their words.
The chief said: " I like to see you all. You look well
—very nice-looking men indeed; but we think you lie,
like all the others. One reason why we don't wish to
sell you the land you want is that we have been much
deceived. When we make treaties for a long time,
we get pretty well paid for a while; but it tapers off
to a very small point, and then we see how completely
we have been cheated. It is plain that you don't
know what you are talking about when you say the
Sioux are going to listen to your words; the Sioux
are dogs—wolves—liars; and you will find it out ere
long."

Not more than an hour after the Indian's speech
the alarm of " Sioux! Sioux! " was given, and in less
than half of a minute not a man was left in the council
lodge—every Indian flew to his gun or bow and ar-

rows, and was off in pursuit of the Sioux. About sunset they returned with five scalps, which they exhibited in front of the store to the gaze of the gentlemanly commissioners. Some of the Indians also had Sioux feet and hands tied around their horses' necks, while old squaws were dancing and jumping upon the scalps. They also took nine horses, but most of them died, having been overfed. "Now," said they, " here are your Sioux; see how well they listen to your words! They are the very same Sioux with whom you have just been making peace. We finished them with the fine new guns you gave them, and scalped them with your own knives. They are the very ones; and you will see some more of them at Fort Rice." [5]

[5] Fort Rice was built on the right bank of the Missouri, 6½ m. above the mouth of the Cannonball, in lat. 46° 31′ N., long. 100° 35′ W. The military reservation was taken from the lands of the Uncpapa or Onkpapa Sioux, on both sides of the river, in what are now Morton and Emmons counties, N. Dak. Building was begun by Col. Dill with six companies of the 30th Wisconsin volunteers July 9, 1864, and the fort was rebuilt in 1868; the location was 300 yards from the river, and 35 feet above low-water mark, immediately above a small " creek on the south," which Lewis and Clark noticed Oct. 18, 1805, and which is now called Long Knife creek. On the opposite side of the Missouri, a mile lower down, is the mouth of Chewah, Shewish, or Fish creek of L. and C., called Shewash by Maximilian in 1833, and now known as Long Lake creek. This stream is mapped as Apple creek by Stevens; but Apple creek is properly the one

DR. WASHINGTON MATTHEWS, U.S.A. (1873.)

The treaty was finally concluded, resulting in the purchase of 15 miles square at Snake river,[6] 16 miles below Fort Berthold, where Fort Stevenson is now standing.[7]

which falls in much higher up, at Sibley island, a few miles from Bismarck. For detailed description of the fort see Dr. Matthews' report, Circ. No. 4, S. G. O., Wash., D. C., 1870, pp. 390-394. This post must not be confounded with present Fort Rice P. O. in Emmons Co., nearly 6 m. higher up in air-line, and much further by water.

[6] So called from certain bluffs known as Loge de Serpent or Snake Den. This small stream flows S. W. into the Missouri, 6 m. by the road below Fort Stevenson: see Henry and Thompson Journs., 1897, p. 320. Snake creek is Miry creek of Lewis and Clark, translating Rivière Bourbeuse of the French: see L. and C., ed. 1893, p. 261. The original name was Mapokshaatiazi, literally Snake House river, so called by the Hidatsa Indians from a sort of cave or hole in the adjacent bluffs where these reptiles were found: *mapoksha*, snake, worm, caterpillar, or other animal offensive to these Indians; *ati*, house; *azi*, river (Matthews, Dict., *s. v.*).

[7] For Forts Berthold and Stevenson, see L. and C., ed. 1893, p. 262 and p. 265. Stevenson was abandoned by the military in the summer of 1883, and turned into an Indian school in the following December. The history of these two places, under military, commercial, and political conditions, and also that of Fort Atkinson, a trading-post, is best given in the article on Stevenson published by Dr. Matthews in the circular above noted, pp. 394-399. He served at both posts as medical officer for some years, making them memorable by the preparation of his Hidatsa Dictionary—a work of the highest authority on the ethnography and philology of those Indians. Dr. Matthews has kindly penned the following special note for the present work:

" The Hidatsa moved up the Missouri from their old village

On the 28th we left Berthold, and next day reached
Rice, where we found, as the Indians had said, the
partisan of the war party, who had been at Berthold;
they were 22 in number.   Further down we stopped
at the Santee Agency, at Running Water [the Nio-

on Knife River to the bluff on which Fort Berthold was afterward
built, in 1845. The Mandans followed them soon after, and the
Arickarees joined them in 1862. Soon after the Hidatsa moved
up, in 1845, the American Fur Co. began, with the assistance
of the Indians, to build a stockaded post, which they called
Fort Berthold in honor of a certain person of that name of
St. Louis. This was built on the extreme southern edge of the
bluff, on land which has since been mostly, if not entirely, cut
away by the river. In 1859 an opposition trading company
erected, close to the Indian village (but east of it and further
away from the river than Fort Berthold), some buildings, protected by stockade and bastions, which they named Fort Atkinson. This was the fort at which Boller served. In 1862 the
opposition ceased, and the A. F. Co. obtained possession of Fort
Atkinson, which they occupied, transferring to it the name of
Fort Berthold. They abandoned the old stockade, which was
afterward (Dec. 24, 1862), almost entirely destroyed by a war
party of Sioux. This was a memorable Christmas eve in the
annals of Berthold. The Sioux came near capturing the post;
but the little citizen garrison defended itself bravely, and at
length the Sioux withdrew. I have heard many stories of this
fight. When I came to Berthold, in the autumn of 1865, there
were one or two houses of hewn logs, occupied by Indians,
standing close to the edge of the bluff, which, I was told, were
the remains of old Fort Berthold. The pictures I have sent you
with the name of Fort Berthold attached represent the structure
which was originally named Fort Atkinson. Like other posts in
the Indian country, it was quadrilateral. Three sides of it were

brara].   The commissioners had a long sitting with
these Indians, who requested them to tell their Great
Father to give them a better place, for they could not
stand it here—no wood, and subject to overflow.
They were afterward removed lower down.   On the

accidentally burned, Oct. 12, 1874.   At the time of this fire and
for some time afterward it was occupied by the United States
Indian Agency.   When the remaining side was abandoned or
when it was razed I do not know.   Within a year I have heard
from there that not a vestige of the old fort or village is left,
except such as the archæologist alone might discover.

" The first (I think) military occupancy of the fort was in 1864,
when Gen. Sully assigned a company of Iowa cavalry to duty
there, under command of Capt. A. B. Moreland.   In the spring
of 1865 this company was relieved by one of the 1st U. S. Vol.
Infantry (ex-Confederate prisoners), under command of Capt.
B. R. Dimon.   In the same year Capt. Dimon's company was
relieved by one of the 4th U. S. Vol. Inf., commanded by Capt.
Adams Bassett.   In the spring of 1866 regular troops came into
the country, and a company of the 13th Infantry, commanded by
Capt. Nathan Ward Osborne (Col. 15th Inf., Aug. 5, 1888, now
deceased), succeeded the volunteers.   When the construction of
Fort Stevenson was begun in 1867 the troops were withdrawn
from Fort Berthold.   When the troops first moved out, the traders
were obliged to move out and build quarters for themselves outside.   After the troops were withdrawn, the traders returned for
a short time; then they made way for the Indian Agency."

The recent status of Berthold was that of an Indian reservation,
agency, mission, etc., where were supplied the temporal and spirit-
ual needs of the once powerful, then decrepit, degenerate, and
mongrelized, Mandans, Arickaras, and Hidatsas, who drew their
rations regularly while they hung in an uncertain balance of
old and new superstitions.   If the latter are superior to the

5th of August we reached Sioux City, where ended the great Peace Commission, and whence all went to their respective homes.

On the 12th of September I lost my daughter—25 years of age. On the 14th of February [1867] my son Charles died, 23 years of age. In the spring I went to St. Louis and made arrangements with the firm of Durfee and Peck to take charge of Union, in opposition to the North West Company. We reached that place on the 19th of June, 1867.[8]

former, these Indians have some hope for this world or the next. The geographic vicissitudes of the place have not been less marked than the ethnographic. When I came to Berthold in 1874 I ran my boat snug under the bluff on which the old village, Berthold, and Atkinson stood, as Lewis and Clark had done Apr. 10, 1805. The agency is now nearly 2 m. lower down, and great sand bars, inclosing a wooded island, besides other made woods on the mainland around the bluff, have pushed the channel of the Missouri a mile or more southward. When the original explorers came by they noticed "a remarkable bend in the river to the southwest," which they called the Little Basin. This is now filled up flush, except a little pond which marks the former bed of the mighty, muddy flood, and is known as Dancing Bear valley—not that bears dance there, or ever did so, but that Indians used to amuse themselves with the ceremony of the Bear Dance, and I suppose do so still. The term is L'Ours qui Danse in French, as used for example by Maximilian, who applies it to hills above the Little Basin; and at least two different creeks in this vicinity, on the same side of the river, have been called Dancing Bear. One of these falls into the Little Basin.

[8] At 2.30 a. m., Wednesday, on the steamer Jennie, which left for Benton at 7 p. m. the same day, according to the Orig. Journ.

According to the request of the gentlemen of this Company, and contrary to my knowledge of the affairs of the concern, I erected an adobe store,[9] 96 by 20 feet. During the summer Colonel Rankin[10] commander of Fort Buford, purchased Fort Union, to use the materials in building Buford. The North West Company then moved down and built at Buford. Finding that all the business of the country would finally be done at Buford, I abandoned my adobe store and erected one there of logs, 120 feet in length. At this place I had to oppose the military sutler and the North West Company. In spite of this I traded 2,000 buffalo robes, 900 elk hides, 1,800 deerskins, and 1,000 wolves', worth, in cash, $5,000; but, owing to some jealousies, malicious reports were

[9] This store of Durfee and Peck was begun on Monday, July 1, and finished Aug. 17. The Orig. Journ. also states that the old kitchen of Fort Union was demolished for fuel on Aug. 4, by the steamer Miner, which arrived that day; that the general demolition of Union was begun by the soldiers on the 7th; and that the journalist moved out of it on the 10th. This ended what may be regarded as on the whole the most historic structure that had ever existed on the Upper Missouri, excepting of course Fort Mandan of Lewis and Clark.

[10] William Galloway Rankin of Pennsylvania, appointed from Washington Territory Captain of the 13th Infantry May 14, 1861; transferred to the 31st Infantry Sept. 21, 1866; brevetted Lieutenant Colonel Mar. 13, 1865, and honorably discharged at his own request Dec. 31, 1870.

made against me, and I was discharged on the arrival
of the steamer, on the 18th of May [1868].[11]

I immediately went to the States, got up an outfit for Indian trade and sutler business, and on the
18th of August [12] I was at Buford again, on my own

[11] Some additional items for May, 1868, in Orig. Journ., are
substantially as follows: 14th. News came in late last night
that two men hauling hay for the Northwest Fur Company had
been killed by the Indians. They were brought in this morning,
being scalped and having each many arrows in their bodies; one
was a negro. They were buried this afternoon. The two spans
of mules as a matter of course were stolen. 20th. A soldier who
cut his throat yesterday was buried this evening with all the
honors of war. The reason he gave for so doing was that he did
not wish to remain any longer in the guardhouse on account of
bad treatment which he received from his officer. 29th. The
steamer Cora brought word that the Amelia Poe had sunk a little
below Milk river; that the Sioux had killed two soldiers and taken
60 head of cattle; and that two citizens had been killed at Round
Butte, by what Indians was unknown. Round Butte stands on
the S. side of the Missouri, 76½ m. by the channel above Milk
river, about halfway between Brown Bear Defeated and Stick
Lodge creek of Lewis and Clark, May 14-17, 1805. The Amelia
Poe was snagged on the 23d about 6 m. by channel below Little
Porcupine or Box Elder creek, and 21 m. below Milk river; details
are given in another note. The Cora here said was No. 3 of that
name, a side-wheeler of 360 tons, owned by Joseph Kinney of
Booneville, Mo.; Capt. Edward Baldwin, pilot, when she was
snagged, Aug. 13, 1869, in Bellefontaine or Cora bend near the
mouth of the Missouri, her wreck causing the formation of Cora
island, Chittenden, Rep. 1897, p. 3877.

[12] After the journalist's discharge from the service of Durfee and
Peck he left the place on the steamer Henry Adkins, June 7, 1868,

hook.   Having made some reductions on all sutler
goods, I acquired popularity among the soldiers, and
did well, considering my small outfit.

On the 3d of June [1869] I went down again and

and reached his home on the Little Sioux on the 18th.   Being determined to return to Buford with an outfit, he sold his farm in
July, and with his brother-in-law, Driggs, raised an equipment
of something like $8,000.   Having left Sioux City on the 29th of
July, he arrived at Buford on the 18th of August, as said in the
text.   The second day after his arrival the journalist started
with a small party on the Yellowstone to cut logs.   On their return in the evening they heard cannon firing at Buford, and on
arrival found that the Sioux had driven off the herd of 210 head
of cattle, and killed three soldiers and wounded several others;
one of the officers, Lieutenant Cusick [Cornelius Charles Cusick,
then of the 31st Infantry] was nearly captured, having been
beaten with clubs; the point of an arrow was sticking in his saddle, and his coming off with his life was considered a miracle.
In consequence of this, the project for building with logs was
abandoned, adobes were made, and on Oct. 13 the store was
opened.   Sales commenced and work went on peaceably till about
the end of that month, when the Indians made a rush on some
soldiers who were shooting prairie chickens.   They killed one
soldier, and left.   Nothing of importance took place till Nov. 20,
when one of the hostile Sioux bragged in camp at the fort of
what he had done in the raid of last summer, when the herd was
driven off.   His boast being reported, he was arrested by Lieutenant Cusick and put into the guardhouse to await trial; but the
third morning he attempted to escape, the guard fired three
shots, and killed him instantly.   This was the last of Mr. Sioux.
(In substance from Orig. Journ.)

Jan. 13, 1869.   It was reported early this morning that a war
party of nine Sioux on horseback intended to revenge the Indian
who had been killed by the guard, and would be likely to make

brought up another outfit the following August.[13] All
went on flourishing with me till the 1st of February,
1870, when I had the misfortune to break my thigh.[14]
    On the 7th of June [1870] I went down to Omaha,
to settle with the firm of Richard Whitney and Co.,
with whom I was concerned. I bought them out,
and returned to Buford.[15] On this trip I was partly

their attack in the forenoon. Some Assiniboines went to look
for their tracks, which they found and followed; they shot one
Sioux off his horse, and got the horse but not the man. The Assiniboines, on the strength of this battle, dug up the Indian who
had been killed by the soldiers, cut him to pieces, scalped him,
and great dances went on in camp. (In substance from Orig.
Journ.)

    [13] We have the Orig. Journ. complete, Jan. 1-June 3, 1869, but I
observe nothing notable during this period. At the latter date it
breaks off, and is not resumed till Aug. 11, 1870. The killing of
four men by the Sioux near Buford, Aug. 10, 1869, may be read
in Joseph H. Taylor's Sketches, etc., Pottstown, Pa., 1889, p. 78
—one of the several incidents of his chapter entitled " Early
Days around Fort Buford." Mr. Taylor is the writer of another
book of similar character, and in both instances appears to have
been his own compositor, proofreader, printer, binder, and publisher, as well as author—not very happily for himself in the case
of any one of these functions. But his productions are not without some merit.

    [14] Dr. Matthews tells me that considerable shortening resulted
from this fracture, and Larpenteur was a cripple ever after.

    [15] Aug. 11, 1870, by Orig. Journ., which resumes at this date,
and continues unbroken during the rest of the year, but with only
daily routine, excepting the matter of the sutlership which the
text proceeds to give briefly. It appears that on Nov. 19, 1870,
Larpenteur mailed his application to the Secretary of War; but

carried by some good folks, who would transport me
from one car to the other, and in hobbling on crutches
I suffered very much. Notwithstanding this great
misfortune, I was getting along pretty well. I had
a splendid establishment at Buford, where I was living with my family, having made it my home. But,
being born for misfortune, I was ruined by the army
bill,[16] which passed Congress the previous July, allow-
ing but one post sutler; this we did not learn till the
following January [1871].[17] My daughter died on the

nothing came of this, as the new sutler had already been appointed. Thus we read at date of Nov. 30 : "The mail arrived
last night bringing news that all the post traders at this place
were to be removed, and one certain individual by the name of
Clayton [that is, Alvin C. Leighton] had been appointed post
sutler."

[16] This was the infamous job which made such a scandal in the
army, such a commotion in Congress, and such a flutter in Washington society, and for which Major General William Worth
Belknap, Secretary of War 1869-76, was justly or unjustly held
responsible. Larpenteur was not the only man ruined; General
Belknap only pretended to hold up his head after that, to the
day of his death. I knew him well, and never believed him
guilty; but this is no place to reopen the case—nor even to
gallantly give *place aux dames*. Cf. Vergil, as cited, note [10],
p. 124.

[17] Jan. 7, 1871. "An express arrived last night from the new
sutler, in consequence of which Larpenteur's and Gerard's stores
were closed," Orig. Journ. They proposed to build at old Fort
Union, but were stopped by orders on the 8th, the military reservation having been extended to 30 miles square. Larpenteur
was permitted to reopen his store Feb. 8, and trade till May 5,

following 14th of February.[18]   On the arrival of the
new post sutler, Mr. Alvin C. Leighton, my store was
closed, like that of the other sutlers.   On the 14th of
May, 1871, I left Buford, bag and baggage, for the
States, and that was the last of the Indian country for
me.[19]

At the time those orders came from headquarters,
I was a regular licensed trader, having been appointed sutler by General Hancock at St. Paul. Notwithstanding that it was in January, we were ordered
forthwith off the reservation, which is only 30 miles

when it was closed, the new sutler having arrived the day before
on the Ida Reese.

[18] So copy, with the almost inexplicable perversion of dates
which characterizes the Autobiography.   The Orig. Journ. for
Feb. 14, 1871, has nothing but a routine item; for Feb. 27 we
read :   " Elizabeth Larpenteur died last night at fifteen minutes
of eleven o'clock and her burial took place at 5 o'clock p. m.   The
weather was very warm."   Compare note [7], p. 175, where I have
already used the correct date.   This daughter had married a discharged soldier named Nott (?).   After her death, Larpenteur
had still a daughter by his last Assiniboine wife; and another
daughter and a boy by his white wife.   The latter daughter
became Mrs. Clowe.   The boy, Louis, soon died, as said beyond.

[19] " May 14, 1871, Sunday.   The Andrew Ackley arrived.   Made
up all the packs and packed up ready to leave for the States in
the morning on the Ackley, who is not to go farther up. . . 15th,
Monday.   Left Buford at 12 precisely."   Orig. Journ. continues
with itinerary of the down voyage, by which it appears that the
boat reached Sioux City on the 21st, and Larpenteur was soon
thereafter at home.

square. Through the kindness of Colonel Gilbert,[20] the commanding officer, we were permitted to remain on the reservation till spring, but our stores were closed. A month afterward we were allowed to open again and go on till the arrival of the regularly appointed sutler. On the 22d of June I took possession of my three forties[21] which I had purchased of the railroad, and built a good house. On the 9th of December my little boy Louis, aged 12 years, died of inflammation of the lungs, after an illness of 48 hours.

Forty years ago was my first winter [1833-34] in the Indian country, at Fort William, when the stars appeared to fall. That my lucky star fell is plainly to be seen in this narrative. Whether there are any such stars may be a question, but there is no question of my being out of luck.[22]

[20] Charles Champion Gilbert of Ohio, then Lieutenant Colonel of the 7th U. S. Infantry.

[21] Three 40-acre lots, or three-fourths of a quarter-section of 160 acres, the section being 640 acres, 1 m. square.

[22] The conclusion of Larpenteur's Autobiography is in sad terms, though set off with his usual show of stoicism. One wonders less at the occasional bitterness, even rancor, which his narrative betrays than at the philosophic pessimism which pervades it, written as it was when he had almost finished the allotted span of life, broken in health, broken in fortune, to die broken-hearted within a year. The manuscript was completed in his home on the Little Sioux, and mailed to Dr. Matthews at Buford, June 14, 1872. His death occurred on the 15th of the following November, as has been already stated.

CHAPTER XX.

AMONG the Blackfeet the law in regard to adultery is death for the adulteress, and forfeiture of all the property of the adulterer. His lodge is cut into pieces, his horses are either killed or taken from him, and the woman must suffer death.

While I was at Benton an instance of this occurred in a very respectable family—for there are such among Indians. I should have said in two families. The woman was very young and handsome. Contrary to custom they had made it up, and the Indian could be seen with his wife as usual; but, being sensible that he had broken the law, he thought that he was looked upon as a weak-hearted man, and could not resist this tormenting idea. She was handsome; he loved her; he must either keep her or kill her. Tortured by reflections, which he could endure no longer, he took her out to walk, as he had been accustomed to do. They were sitting together, when he took her on his lap, combed her hair neatly,—which is a mark of love with all Indians,—vermilioned her face beautifully, and told her to sit by his side again. He then said, " My good wife, you have done wrong. I thought at one time I could overlook it, but I am scorned by my people.   I cannot suffer you to be the wife of another.   I love you too much for that. You must die."   So saying, he buried his tomahawk in her skull.

When an Indian sees that his wife makes too free with young men, the penalty for such an offense is a piece of the nose.   I have seen several who have undergone that punishment, and awful did they look. After cutting off her nose the husband says, " Go now and see how fond the young men will be of talking to you."

Among the Assiniboines there is no particular law in regard to adultery.   This is left at the disposition of the injured individual, who sometimes revenges himself; but, if the relatives of the adulterer are strong, he may be content with a payment.   Some give the woman a flogging, and then either drive her away or keep her.   Nothing will be said about it, but the woman then bears a bad name—in their language Wittco Weeon,[1] which means a prostitute, but not one of the first degree.   A regular prostitute has no husband, and goes about to " lend herself," as they term it, for pay.   Such a woman is gone beyond re-

[1] *Witkowin*—literally, " fool woman."

demption.   There are three different degrees of pros-
titution, one of which is looked upon as legal.   This
is when she is loaned with the consent of her parents,
and then the larger the payment the more honor it is
for the woman.   When little quarrels arise among
mothers in regard to the characters of their daugh-
ters, they will say, " What have you to say against
my daughter?   What did yours get when you lent
her?   Look at mine—what she got!   You are making a Wittico Weeon of your daughter."

The young man who is courting dresses himself
in the best style he can afford.   His hair, which is the
main point of attraction, is generally well combed in
front, taking care that his stiff topknot stands straight
up, while a long braid of false hair hangs down to his
heels.   With large pieces of California shells [abalone
—*Haliotis*] in his ears, his neck and breast covered
with an immense necklace of beads, his face vermilioned, and a fine pair of moccasins on his feet, his
dress is complete.   His over garment is either a blanket or a robe.   Attired in this style, he commences
his courtship by standing quite still in a place where
he thinks that she will be likely to see him.   This
may last for many days without saying a word to her.
He then makes friends with her brothers, particularly
the elder one, who has a great deal to say in regard
to the marrying of his sister.   Then he watches for her

when she goes for wood or water, saying a few words to her, and giving her a finger ring. When he makes small presents to the mother, father, and brothers they discover what he is after; but he never enters the lodge of his sweetheart. At this stage of the proceedings, if the young couple get very much in love with each other, and the young man cannot obtain the means to buy her, they elope to another band of the same tribe. But if he be a young man of means, and has obtained the consent of the woman, he ties a horse at her lodge; if the horse is accepted, the girl goes that night to his lodge; if not, the horse remains tied at the lodge, and the young man sends for it in the morning. If he has other horses, and loves the girl enough, the following day he ties two; and sometimes four or five horses are thus tied—the more horses, the greater honor for all parties. An elopement may also take place when the old folks will not consent, after the girl has been given the refusal of a horse. She is never forced to marry. Sometimes the individual who wants to buy a girl has never asked her whether she would have him or not, but has made very inducing offers to her parents, who then do all they can to persuade her, saying, " Take pity on us, daughter! This man likes us. He has given us a great many things. We are poor; we stand much in need of horses. He is a good hunter; he will make you live well; you need not remain poor." Yet, if the girl does not consent, they will not force her.

After marriage the woman belongs to the man. No one else has any right to her; and if she be the eldest, and have two or three sisters, they are also considered his wives, and cannot be disposed of without his consent. It frequently happens that he will take them all. The son-in-law never speaks to or looks at either of his parents-in-law. When invited to a feast or council where his father-in-law is to be he is duly apprised of it, and he covers himself with his robe and turns his back upon the old gentleman. An Indian who has but one wife will always be poor; but one that has three to four wives may become rich— one of the leading men, if not a chief. The reason of this is that the more wives the more children, and children are a source of wealth, resulting in a large family connection, which gives him power; for " might makes right " with them. An Indian marries also in this light: When his family has increased with one wife till they find it impossible to get along without help, he buys a servant, as there is no such thing as hiring one; but she also becomes his wife, and is not looked upon as a servant. In all cases the old wife is always looked up to as the mistress of the whole. The son-in-law never keeps anything to himself until he gets a family; everything goes to his

wife's relations, and this may continue even after he
has a considerable family. From such customs it is
plainly to be seen that the more wives an Indian has
the richer he is—contrary to what the case may be
with the whites. Notwithstanding customs so
strange to us, these Indians live as peaceably and con-
tentedly as civilized people do. It is a fine sight to
see one of those big men among the Blackfeet, who
has two or three lodges, five or six wives, twenty or
thirty children, and fifty to a hundred head of horses;
for his trade amounts to upward of $2,000 a year,
and I assure you such a man has a great deal of dig-
nity about him.

The medicine lodge, which takes place once a year,
in June, is conducted with the view to show how
strong are Indians' hearts, and to beg the Great
Spirit to have mercy upon the tribe. This lodge is
erected of a size suitable to hold whatever number of
spectators may be in attendance. A very large pole
is planted in the ground, and many smaller ones are
set up against it, in the manner of an ordinary lodge.
One half of the space inside is reserved for those who
are to undergo the torture, of which there are three
kinds. In this half of the lodge pews are made with
green bushes about four feet high; those for the
women being separated from the others. When all
is ready for the services to commence, the supposed

strong-hearted persons come in and take their stands. They are painted in all colors, looking like so many devils—men and women alike; the former are naked down to their waists, but the latter are dressed. Holding in their mouths a small whistle made of the bone of a crow or pelican, and looking straight up to the center post of the lodge, they keep whistling and jumping up and down for three days and three nights, without drinking or eating; during which time eight or ten musicians, all blackened over, beat drums the whole night and day.

The second torture is done by piercing a hole through the skin of each breast, just above the nipple, and tying to each a lariat, which is then fastened by the other end to the top of the lodge-pole. Bearing all the weight they can upon the lariat, they trot back and forth outside the lodge, the space allowed each being according to the number of performers. This kind of torture goes on with a piteous groaning and lamentation, and these devotees are also painted in all sorts of colors, like the dancers. The third medicine or torture is performed by piercing a hole in each shoulder, to which lariats are fastened as before, but the other ends are tied to three or four dry buffalo skulls, which the communicant drags over the prairie, sometimes even up to high ridges, weeping and wailing. Such performances are a great sight to behold.

An Indian chief is looked upon by most civilized people as a powerful and almost absolute ruler of his tribe; but he is not. Every tribe, no matter how small, is divided into bands, each of which has its chief and roams in a different part of the territory belonging to the tribe. As everything must have a head, a chief is appointed to represent the band in councils with the whites, and be consulted in the way of governing. He is a man who has power to do a great deal of harm, but as a general thing does little good. The soldier is the one who governs the band, and rules the chief, too, with a kind of government which the civilians do not like; for when the soldier is established, they are under martial law. His lodge, pitched in the center of the camp, is organized with the view to keep order and regulate the camp; mostly to prevent anyone from going out alone on a hunt, so as not to raise the buffalo, but also for mutual protection against enemies. When anyone is caught outside his dogs are shot, his lodge is cut to pieces, and if he rebels he gets a pounding—the chief not excepted. Those soldiers have their head soldier, to whom each one applies to have his rights respected or enforced. If anything be stolen, the head soldier is apprised of the theft; he takes some of the soldiers to examine the lodges, and if the property is found it is given back to the owner, but nothing is done

with the thief. This lodge is supported by the people, who have to find wood, water, and meat. Buffalo tongues go mostly to the soldiers' lodge, and, if
there be more than can be eaten, they are sent to be
traded for sugar, coffee, and flour to make a big feast.
But the regular soldiers' feast is dog, and when they
feel like having such, no poor old squaw's fine, fat,
young dogs are spared. Take it on the whole, Indians are very glad when the lodge breaks up, and each
one can go where he pleases. After that the chief
will be left with eight or ten lodges, as they then go
by those family connections which make leading men,
some of whom actually have more influence than the
chief himself—I mean with the people of the band.

All things considered, an educated man will see
that their whole system of government amounts to
nothing; that they are incapable of enforcing any laws
like those of a civilized nation, and consequently not
able to comply with treaties made with the United
States. But such laws as they have answer their
own purposes. As a nation they are kind and good
to one another, and live in about as much peace and
comfort as civilized people—that is, in their own way.
One hears less complaint about hard times among
them than among ourselves, except when they make
a speech to a white man; then they are all very poor
and pitiful, on the begging order. As a general

thing the men are not quarrelsome. A fight will take
place almost without a word. The women quarrel
a good deal, and frequently fight with knives or
clubs.

There are men and women doctors among them.
They use some kinds of herbs and roots, but their
greatest medical reliance is the magic of superstition.
When the doctor is sent for, he comes with his drum,
and a rattle, made of a gourd or dry hide filled with
gravel. He sits beside the patient, and commences to
beat the drum and shake the rattle at a great rate,
singing a kind of song, or rather mumbling some
awful noise. He always finds out what ails the patient. Sometimes it is a spell which has been thrown
on him by some medicine man in camp, who had a
spite against him. Such spells vary. Sometimes
they are cords which have been passed through the
limbs; at other times wolf hairs have been put between the skin and flesh, or bird claws of different
kinds. But all of these he extracts by his magic, and
shows the patient the hairs, claws, cords, or whatever
may have been the spell. But some maladies are due
to the devil, who has got into the sick person. In
a case of that kind the doctor stations three or four
boys with loaded guns outside the lodge at night;
then he beats his drum at an awful rate, and at a certain sound, which is understood by the boys, they

fire off their guns at the ground, as though they were shooting at rats running out of the lodge. These are supposed to be the devils whom the doctor has driven out of his patient. Should he continue sick, the treatment is repeated until he is cured or given up. Indians spare nothing to have their families or themselves doctored; they will give their guns, lodges, horses—everything they possess—to a doctor who will cure them. I have seen some completely stripped of all they had to pay the doctor. When a child dies the parents give everything away to mourners; and if the family is rich there will be a great many mourners, particularly among the women, who come to shed a few tears for the sake of plunder. It is thought, " She cries; she loved my child; she must have something." The mourning lasts for a year, unless some relation kills one of their enemies; then the family blacken their faces, which does away with the period of mourning. After this, someone will give a gun, another a horse, some other a lodge, and thus the Indian will get a start again.

Medicine men who are thought able to lay spells are much in danger, and sometimes lose their lives at the hands of the relations of one who dies by such magic. I myself saw a young man kill a fine-looking Indian for having, as he said, laid a spell on his father, who died of consumption. The young man shot him at night, about twenty steps from the fort. We went to see him in the morning; he was lying dead, the ball having penetrated his heart. The young man was there, laughing and whirling his tomahawk over him, saying, " That doctor will lay no more spells."

Indians have no words for swearing or cursing, like whites, but they have a way to express wrath a great deal more scornfully than a white man can in words. This is done by gathering the four fingers against the thumb and letting them spring open, at the same time throwing out the arm, straight in one's face, with the body and face half turned away, saying, " Warchteshnee," [2] which means, as nearly as I can interpret it, " You villain! "

The Indian idea of futurity and immortality of the soul is something about which I never could find out much.[3] All Indians believe in a Great Spirit, the ruler of all they see and know, but of any future existence, in which the wicked are punished and the good rewarded, they know nothing. They believe in ghosts, who live again in an invisible form, thinking that their dead relations come to see them; and

[2] Literally, " no good "; *washté*, good, and *shni* = negative, no.
[3] But any priest who understands his business can find out in forty winks, and explain in forty pages of print, what Larpenteur failed to discover in forty years. It takes all sorts of doctors, including such divines as Larpenteur has described, besides other kinds of people, to make the world go round.

that the only way ghosts make themselves known is
by whistling, mostly at night, but sometimes by day,
in very lonesome places.   In consequence of this be-
lief, they make feasts for the ghosts, consisting principally of dried berries, which they would not for anything omit to gather.   They boil these berries with
meat, or pound a quantity of buffalo meat with marrow fat, with either of which they go to the place
where the dead is deposited, say a few words to the
departed, hold the eatables up for him or her to
partake of, and then divide the feast among the living who are in attendance.   Anyone is allowed to
attend this ceremony.   But whether the ghosts are
in a state of happiness or not, they do not pretend to
say, nor do they know what distinction may be made
between the good and the wicked.   To themselves
it makes no difference; they feed both good and bad
alike.

On being very hard pressed for a statement ex-
pressing their ideas regarding resurrection, most Indians would finally say that they thought once dead
was the last of a person.   In conversation with them
I found much pleasure in hearing their stories, which
they relate with great eloquence, using a great many
figurative expressions.   I had some books printed in
their language, which I brought with me from St.
Paul.   These were religious books, gotten up by mis-

sionaries of Minnesota, containing Noah's Ark, Jonah swallowed by the whale, and other miracles; at which they would laugh heartily when I read to them, and then say, " Do the whites believe all this rub-bish, or are they stories such as we make up to amuse ourselves on long winter nights? " They were very fond of having me read them such stories; that big boat tickled them, and how could Noah get all those animals into it was the question. Then they would say, " The white man can beat us in making up stories." Telling stories is a great pastime with In-dians. There are many among them who are good at it; they are always glad to see such come into a company, saying, " Here is such a one; now we'll have some stories told."

The Indian is born, bred, and taught to be a war-rior and a hunter; he aspires to nothing else. There is no regular habit of husbandry among them; they always live from hand to mouth. During the 40 years I was in their country I saw no disposition on their part to ameliorate their condition. They are still in the same state. They have no intellectual invention.   In regard to their " medicine," one per-formance which has attracted my attention I do not attribute to magic but to skill. This is the way in which they bring a band of buffalo into their pens. Such a pen is constructed of poles, and bushes, and

any other combustibles they can obtain to make a
kind of fence, which is by no means sufficient to keep
in the buffalo. This inclosure is made of different
sizes, but is generally capable of containing 200 or
300 buffaloes. It is made round, and a pole is stuck
up in the middle, with scarlet cloth, kettles, pans,
and a great many other articles tied to the top.
Those are sacrifices to the Great Spirit, made by the
individual who is to go after the buffalo. When this
pen is finished two wings are made extending a great
distance from the entrance, like an immense quail
net. These wings are made either of snow or of buffalo chips, gathered at intervals into small heaps sufficiently large to conceal a person. As the pen must
be made where there is little wood, it frequently happens that the buffalo are discovered two or three days'
march from the spot. When all is ready, the medicine man starts after the buffalo. When the people
of the camp see him coming, they all surround the
pen, except those who are stationed at intervals along
the wings, each hidden behind a pile of snow or chips.
The buffalo follow him, and when the last one has
passed, the herd being completely within the wings,
the people all rise from their places of concealment.
The buffalo then rush into the pen. Then the people
who surround the pen also rise up, and are joined by
those who were behind the wings. The buffalo, be-

ing frightened, keep away from the sides of the pen, running around the pole in the middle; though it sometimes happens that, the pen being too small or too weak, they break through in spite of all the Indians can do. With their bows and arrows the Indians begin the work of destruction, and go on till all the buffalo are killed. It is a good sight to see that one Indian bring in a large band of buffalo, which has followed him for two or three days. He is considered a great medicine man.

CHAPTER XXI.

BEFORE offering some suggestions I wish to make in regard to future rules and regulations for Indians and their country, I will introduce all the Indian agents I have personally known on the Missouri. In 1832 Major Sanford took from Union to Washington three chiefs—one Assiniboine, one Cree, and one Chippewa. The Assiniboine was the son of the chief of the Rock or Stone band, named Wan-hee-manza[1] (the Iron Arrow-point). He was a fine-looking man about 30 years of age, named Lya-jan-jan[2]

[1] *Wanhi*, a flake of flint, arrowhead ; and *maza*, metal.

[2] This is the Indian whom Catlin gives under another name, with portrait and that of his wife, plates 28 and 29. The account occupies pp. 55 and 56 of the 4th London ed. i, 1844, in part as follows : " I have painted the portrait of a very distinguished young man, and son of the chief (plate 28); his dress is a very handsome one. . . The name of this man is Wi-jun-jon (the pigeon's egg head) and by the side of him (plate 29) will be seen the portrait of his wife, Chin-cha-pee (the fire bug that creeps), a fine-looking squaw. . . I have just had the satisfaction of seeing this travelled-gentleman (Wi-jun-jon) meet his tribe, his wife and his little children ; after an absence of a year or more,

(the Shining Man). All the manners and other good things which he brought from Washington, to show his people what an advance he had made in civilization, was a white towel, which he used to wipe his face and hands, and a house-bell, which he tied to the door of his lodge. His people said that all he had got from the whites was a gift of the gab. After his return he passed himself off for a great medicine man, and said that no ball could penetrate his skin. He had a strong connection, and was much feared. But the next summer a certain individual thought he would try the strength of his medicine, and shot a bullet through his head. The ball was harder than his head, and went through in spite of the strength of

on his journey of 6000 miles to Washington City, and back again (in company with Major Sanford, the Indian agent); where he has been spending the winter amongst the fashionables in the polished circles of civilized society. . . On his way home from St. Louis to this place, a distance of 2000 miles, I traveled with this gentleman, on the steamer Yellow-Stone; and saw him step a shore (on a beautiful prairie, where several thousands of his people were encamped), with a complete suit *en militaire*, a colonel's uniform of blue, presented to him by the President of the United States, with a beaver hat and feather, with epaulettes of gold—with sash and belt, and broad sword; with high-heeled boots—with a keg of whiskey under his arm, and a blue umbrella in his hand." Again, in vol. ii, pp. 194–200, Catlin takes occasion to embroider the " Story of Wi-jun-jon " in retelling it, and to introduce his plates 271, 272. These are among the most effective of his whole series, and they point such a moral, besides so adorning the tale, that I need not apologize for reproducing them.

his medicine.   He was brought to Fort Union, and
buried after their own way in a tree.   In the summer
a requisition for Indian skulls was made by some
physicians from St. Louis.   His head was cut off and
sent down in a sack with many others.[3]   Which of

[3] Orig. Journ. has in substance at date of Sunday, Sept. 13,
1835, another case whose sequel furnishes a parallel instance :
" About eleven o'clock we were suddenly informed by a squaw
that La Vache Blanche, who had been sick for some time, had
stuck an arrow in his heart, and that his wife desired some of us
to come and pull it out.   On entering his lodge with the interpreter I found him lying on his back dead, still holding in his left
hand the arrow, the feathered part of which had been broken off,
leaving about six inches of the shaft sticking out of the wound.
Pulling on this I succeeded in withdrawing it till the head reached
the skin, but was obliged to cut the skin to extract the head.
I was informed that some time ago he said he had suffered long
enough, and knowing that he must die he intended to take his
own life.   The family applied to Mr. Hamilton for a blanket to
cover the body, and it was buried in a tree, Indian fashion."
What finally became of White Cow's skull is told in the following
extract from Audubon's Journ., ii, 1897, p. 72, at date of July 2,
1843 : " Mr. Denig and I walked off with a bag and instruments,
to take off the head of a three-years-dead Indian chief, called the
White Cow.   Mr. Denig got on my shoulders and into the branches
near the coffin, which stood about ten feet above ground.   The
coffin was lowered, or rather tumbled, down, and the cover was
soon hammered off ; to my surprise, the feet were placed on the
pillow, instead of the head, which lay at the foot of the coffin—
if a long box may be so called.   Worms innumerable were all
about it; the feet were naked, shrunk, and dried up.   The head
had still the hair on, but was twisted off in a moment, under jaw
and all.   The body had been first wrapped up in Buffalo skin

them came out first is hard to tell; but I don't think his did. This is the whole amount of good that chief did. As he went down during President Jackson's administration, his name, with the whites, was Jackson. The Cree chief never amounted to anything, nor did the Chippewa.

Major Sanford was very much of a gentleman, but cared more for the interests of the American Fur Company than for Indian affairs. He afterward married Mr. Pierre Chouteau's daughter,[4] and one can judge in whose favor his reports would be likely to be made.

without hair, and then in another robe with the hair on, as usual ; after this the dead man had been enveloped in an American flag, and over this a superb blanket. We left all on the ground but the head. Squires, Mr. Denig and young Owen McKenzie went afterwards to try to replace the coffin and contents in the tree, but in vain ; the whole affair fell to the ground, and there it lies; but I intend to-morrow to have it covered with earth. The history of this man is short, and I had it from Mr. Larpenteur, who was in the fort at the time of his decease, or self-committed death. He was a good friend to the whites, and knew how to procure many Buffalo robes for them ; he was also a famous orator, and never failed to harangue his people on all occasions. He was, however, consumptive, and finding himself about to die, he sent his squaw for water, took an arrow from his quiver, and thrusting it into his heart, expired, and was found dead when his squaw returned to the lodge. He was ' buried ' in the above mentioned tree by the order of Mr. McKenzie, who then commanded this fort."

[4] Emilie Chouteau, eldest daughter of Pierre Chouteau, Jr., and Emilie Gratiot, b. Feb. 13, 1814, married John F. A. Sanford.

Major Ferguson, the greenest of all agents I ever saw, was paid $1,500 for a pleasure trip from St. Louis to Fort Union. He came up in the steamer, saw no Indians, and left what few annuities he had to be divided among them by the Company. What report could that agent make in regard to his Indians? None, of course. That was the last of him.

Major More was a great drunkard, who came up to Union in the steamer, remained 24 hours, and returned to Fort Pierre. It was reported by a person whom I believe, that the Indians there kicked his stern, taking him for a dog, when he was crawling out of the room where they had been sleeping, and laughingly said they were very sorry that they had kicked their father.

Major Matloch was a drunken gambler. The last I saw of him was at Trader's Point, opposite Bellevue, where he was drinking and gambling, and kept several Mormon women. I was informed that he died, shortly afterward, in poverty.

Major Dripps[5] was, I believe, a good, honest old beaver trapper. He was sent to examine the trading posts, to find out about the liquor trade. He sent

[5] Andrew Dripps, an early trader, long associated with Lucien Fontenelle under the firm name of Fontenelle and Dripps. He was an Indian agent in 1843, when Audubon met him as such near Fort Vermilion, en route down from Fort Pierre with Wm. Laidlaw, May 18: see his Journ. i, 1897, p. 499.

his interpreter ahead to let us know he was coming. On his arrival he looked in all places except in the cellar, where there was upward of 30 barrels of alcohol. The major was afterward equipped by the American Fur Company, and went on the Platte, where he died.

Major Hatting was a young man about 27 or 28 years old, a drunkard and a gambler, almost gone up by the bad disorder. He was of no earthly account. I could say much more, but decency forbids.

Major Norwood, instead of being with his Indians, kept himself about Sergeant's Bluffs, attending balls and parties given by whites and half-breeds, and was finally killed by William Thompson, who knocked his brains out with the butt of a rifle. This was the last of the major.

Major Redfield [9] went 50 miles up the Yellowstone, on his way to the Crows, was taken sick, and returned to the States in the fall; his goods were left to be divided by the Company. I knew nothing regarding his personal character.

Major Vaughan was a jovial old fellow, who had a very fine paunch for brandy, and, when he could not

[9] Major Redfield ascended the Missouri in the Twilight, Capt. John Shaw, which left St. Louis May 23, 1858. This was the boat which took Boller up, and he has much to say of the major in his book, p. 24, *seq*.

get brandy, would take almost anything which would make drunk come. He was one who remained most of his time with his Indians, but what accounts for that is the fact that he had a pretty young squaw for a wife; and as he received many favors from the Company, his reports must have been in their favor.

I have but little to say about Major Schoonover, who remained one winter at Union, powerless, like all others, being dependent on the American Fur Company.

Major Latta was a pretty fair kind of a man, but the less said of him the better. He came up to Union, put the annuities out on the bar, and next day was off.

Major Mahlon Wilkinson came as near doing the right thing as was in his power, but he was too lazy to do much of anything.

Major Clifford[7] was a captain of the regular army, which rendered him unfit for such an office, not caring a fig about Indians. I could say a great deal

[7] Walter Clifford of New York rose from the ranks to be second lieutenant of the 16th Infantry Aug. 10, 1863, and first lieutenant May 14, 1864; he was transferred to the 34th Infantry Sept. 21, 1866, and promoted to be captain July 31, 1867; he was on detached service from Apr. 14, 1869, to Jan. 1, 1871, when he was assigned to the 7th Infantry. He was brevetted for gallant and meritorious service at the battle of Chickamauga, and died Feb. 23, 1883. Larpenteur is unfair to this officer, who always tried to do his best.

more if I felt so disposed. From what I have been
able to learn I fully believe that all the Indian agents
were of the same material; and had those men been
ever so well qualified to fill their office, they could
not have done it under the existing rules and regulations. Once in the Indian country they came entirely
under the influence of the American Fur Company,
and could not help themselves.

Those gentlemen were appointed by the Indian Department not only as agents, but as fathers to the
Indians; to remain with their children, and to make
true reports to their Great Father at Washington of
the behavior of the Indians and of all transactions in
their country that come to the agent's notice, thus
keeping the department well posted. The question
is, Was that done? No; evidence shows the contrary.
In consequence of this bad state of affairs, the department remained ignorant of the true condition of
the country, and could never hold the proper kind of
council with the Indians; and, finally, war broke out.
Of all the councils I attended, I never saw one properly held, according to my knowledge of Indian character and customs.

I will mention one, which was the most absurd I
ever heard of—though gotten up by men who should
have known better. This is the Laramie treaty of
1851.

David D. Mitchell, who had been an Indian trader, was the superintendent of Indian affairs at St. Louis. I suppose speculation, as in the case of all other treaties, was the cause of this one. It was gotten up with the intention of making a general peace between all the tribes on the Missouri and the Platte. For this purpose two or three chiefs of each tribe were invited to the treaty. Anyone who has the least knowledge of Indian character ought to know that they are not capable of keeping such a peace. Of course any Indian, for the sake of presents, will say " How " to any proposition made to him; but, after that, what assurance have you to rely upon that this Indian will comply with the stipulations of the treaty? None at all. You may say that, if he does not comply, he shall forfeit a part of his annuities. But if you make him forfeit his annuities it will be worse; for, although this will have been explained to him, he will think that he had a right to do as he did. He will say that his young men had no ears; that he did all in his power, but could not control them; and still think himself entitled to the annuities. He will surely find some excuse.

The result of the Laramie treaty was that the Indians fought before they got home; war was carried on among them the same as before, and afterward war with the whites. At the time of this treaty, did the Crows think the Sioux would be permitted by the Government, after all the promises made them, to drive away their traders from the Yellowstone, and that they themselves would then be driven out of their own country? Did Crazy Bear, chief of the Assiniboines, expect his people to be removed from their country into that of their enemies? "No," they said, "the whites have lied to us. They have taken our country. They say they bring soldiers to protect us; but, when they come, they bring the Sioux with them. Loads of provisions come out of their garrisons for the Sioux, who are on our own lands, and we can get nothing. Do they give rations to the Sioux because they are afraid of them, or is it because the Sioux drive away their cattle and kill their soldiers? We cannot understand those whites. We had a good country, which we always thought they would save for us; they have given it to our enemies. Fort Union, the house built for our old fathers,—in the heart of our country,—the soldiers have pulled it down to build their Fort Buford, where we are scarcely permitted to enter."

It is plainly to be seen that treaties made with Indians have never amounted to anything, and never will. The Government must manage them; but, to do so, must be well acquainted with their wants. They are called children, and must be treated as such.

The father should know his children; but how can he know them if he is not with them? And if he be a worthless father, how can he bring up his children right? My suggestions will show the proper way to manage Indians. I think I have plainly shown errors in the Indian Department. Treaties, councils, and expeditions have not had the desired effect.

One not acquainted with Indians might say that the army has been the means of bringing them under some subjection. I know that the chief motive for yielding was not the sword, the bullet, or the bayonet, but hunger and the prospect of starvation. Had the Indians continued to possess the buffalo which were theirs 25 years ago, a different display of armed forces would have been made. Hunger has somewhat tamed them, much against their will. When I first came into the country few Indians liked coffee, and they looked at a white man's eating pork as we did an Indian's eating dog.

It must be borne in mind that the Indian is wild, and that any attempt to tame him is going entirely contrary to his nature. The question remains with me, can it be done? From what I have seen, and knowing him as I do, I would say it cannot be done; yet there is nothing like trying. The following suggestions are those I propose for the trial. In the first place, much of the Indian country is not capable

of large settlements, on account of the insuscepti-
bility of the soil for agriculture, and the scarcity of
timber. I would divide the tribes into agencies according to their population, and establish regularly
surveyed boundaries to each of those agencies. In
all tribes in which there were more than one agent,
I would have a superintendent, who should be called
the governor of the tribe. All agents should be obliged
to remain nine months in the year at their agencies.
They should keep a regular diary of all transactions,
and a regular list of chiefs and leading men of the
tribe, stating their characters and giving all such other
information as would tend to bring them to the ac-
quaintance of his successor. In tribes where there
was but one agency, this agent should be the governor of the entire tribe, and have the power to issue
a license for trading with Indians or whites to any
American citizen, without bonds. This agency
should be the point where all business should be trans-
acted. No traders or storekeepers should be allowed
to establish themselves more than 500 yards from the
agency, and under no consideration should they be
permitted to go among the Indians to trade. Every
trader and storekeeper should be provided with the
rules and regulations of the agency, and, should he
violate any of them, his store should be closed, and
himself ordered out of the country, never to be al-

lowed to trade again in any of the Indian countries. No white man should be allowed to live with a squaw for a wife, unless lawfully married; and such marriage should entitle him to the same privileges as an Indian. The agent should be allowed 25 laboring men, two carpenters, one wheelwright, one blacksmith, one engineer, and one sawyer. All laborers should be enlisted for the term of two years, under military rules and regulations, but allowed to dress as they pleased. A laundress should be provided by the department for the benefit of the men, her wages to be $30 per month. The amount of washing allowed at this rate to each man per week should be two shirts, one pair of drawers, two pair of socks, and two handkerchiefs; all fine linen shirts to be paid for extra. Laborers should receive $30 per month, paid every two months. No house should be frame, but all built of sawed or hewn logs, roofed with earth, having pine floors, doors, and casings for windows and doors.

The agent or governor should have full control over the territory said to belong to his Indians. To give him power to enforce rules and regulations and to police his territory well, I would recommend a military post of one or more companies, according to the Indian population, to be established not over half a mile from the agency. The troops should be cavalry, as infantry avails naught in the Indian coun-

try. The commander of such a post should have
nothing to do with Indians, being only stationed
there to assist and protect the governor, and should
never be permitted to act without the latter's consent.

This governor should be provided with all kinds of
agricultural implements, to be distributed to his Indians. He should furnish them with timber to build
and allow them each a certain sum in payment for
every panel of fence any Indian might put up, besides
furnishing him with material to make it; and so much
an acre for breaking his land, let it be with the plow or
hoe. All fences should be horse-high, bull-strong,
and hog-tight. Hogs, cattle, and chickens should be
distributed, and there should be an agricultural fair
annually, as in the States. Every three months in-
spect the Indian houses, and give premiums to the
first, second, and third best housekeeper. Hold
monthly meetings with chiefs and leading men, and as
many others as the house can hold. There are many
other regulations I could suggest, but the above are
the main ones. Agencies being established in this
manner, the agent cannot fail to be well posted on
the state of affairs in his territory, and can thus
govern with due care.

In regard to schools and missions I think that the
Indians are still too wild for any such establishments

or institutions. They must first be turned to agriculture, be taught habits of industry and economy, and thus become gradually accustomed to the ways of the whites. It would be better, in my opinion, to postpone the institutions for a few years. Teach them the Ten Commandments, and try to make them obey them—which I leave for the governor to do if he can. There are two strong obstacles to success—the wild nature of the Indians, and the sterility of their soil.

To secure an agent or a governor fit for such an office would require a salary of at least $3,000 a year, instead of $1,500.

After all, whether agencies be established in this manner or not, I see no use of the military posts now on the Missouri. I do not propose to abolish them with the view of saving expense to the Government, but rather to apply the military to the work of ameliorating the condition of the Indian. Supposing agencies established as I have suggested, what would be the use of Randall, Sully, Rice, Stevenson, and Buford? To my knowledge they have never been of any use. They have reservations 30 miles square, upon which no one is allowed to remain but themselves, their sutler, and contractor; and that land is generally taken from the best part of the Indian country. Thus stationed, far apart, with infantry only, what good do they do? Whom have they to protect but themselves? From Berthold to Peck, a distance of at least 500 miles, there are no agencies, nor traders. Buford is situated about the middle of this distance, with three or four companies of infantry. What are they there for but to do nothing on the best of the land at the greatest expense? Stevenson is perfectly useless. Rice is situated where no Indians go, 125 miles from Stevenson, and about the same distance from Grand River agency; of what use is it, with its four companies? None. Sully is in sight of the Cheyenne agency, with one or two companies, and all the organized agencies below. I pronounce it of no earthly use. Randall ditto. The country will not support such large garrisons. The scarcity of grass and fuel will not admit of such forts, which destroy the best locations on the river and displease the Indians to no purpose. Buford has one of the best locations, which would answer for a very extensive Indian reservation; there is not another such point on the river between Randall and Benton. It is now spoiling that fine country for the mere sake of living there.

On these large military reservations no licensed Indian traders are allowed; but the sutler is allowed to trade with Indians, and they are permitted to come on the reservation. If a licensed trader wishes to establish a post he cannot do so nearer than 15 miles from the garrison, much too far to receive any protection, and this gives the sutler the monopoly of the Indian trade. As the soldier trade is well secured, it is plainly to be seen that the military rule the Indian country. But my suggestions would put the control of the Indian and his country where it properly belongs.

If the Indians should commit depredations requiring punishment, would those garrisons, organized as they are now, be able to pursue and chastise them? Surely not; and, if they had absolutely to be punished, the government would have to send a different force after them, and let the garrisons eat their pork and beans uselessly, as usual.

A few days after writing my remonstrance in regard to the garrisons on the Missouri, I saw in the Sioux City Journal a report made by a gentleman named A. D. Rodefer, in reference to the pastimes of the officers of Fort Rice. During his stay at the post he participated in a deer-hunt with the officers. There are sixteen hounds at the fort, and a number of experienced hunters; and what with the hunters and the hounds, the officers' tables are constantly supplied with game. The amusements at Rice are numerous and varied. Two nights in the week the post is entertained by amateur theatrical and minstrel troupes. One night is devoted to dancing, and the rest to epicurean parties, etc.

Such reports, I think, show the uselessness of these garrisons. Why do the soldiers not amuse themselves by running after this famous Sitting Bull, who, the same reporter says, is bound to take Fort Peck this winter? No; they would freeze. It is best for them to dance all winter, and let the United States send somebody else after Sitting Bull when the grass grows in the spring.

Ta-tang-ah-eeoting's [8] or Sitting Bull's ideas in regard to the whites were expressed in my presence at Fort Union in 1867. He remarked: " I have killed, robbed, and injured too many white men to believe in a good peace. They are medicine, and I would eventually die a lingering death. I had rather die on the field of battle "—or, as he put it—" have my skin pierced with bullet holes." " And, for another thing," he continued, " I don't want to have anything to do with people who make one carry water on the shoulders and haul manure." He has frequently invited the Sioux and Assiniboines to join him, telling them not to stick so close to the whites, getting as poor as snakes, eating nothing but bacon

[8] Commonly written Tatanka Iyotanka; from *tatánka*, a bull bison, and *iyotanka*, to sit; but *iyotankahan* is the participle, sitting.

and hard-tack. They had better leave, he thought, and do as he did—go into the buffalo country, eat plenty of meat, and when they wanted a good horse, go to some fort and steal one. " Look at me," he said; " see if I am poor, or my people either. The whites may get me at last,° as you say, but I will have good times till then. You are fools to make yourselves slaves to a piece of fat bacon, some hard-tack, and a little sugar and coffee."

° Sitting Bull was a prophet, no doubt, but no extraordinary sagacity was required to foresee this. During the excitement aroused by the ghost-dances still fresh in the public mind, he was killed Dec. 15, before the affair of Wounded Knee, Dec. 29, 1890. In the course of his long career of professional scoundrelism and criminality, he probably made more mischief and did more damage than any other contemporary Indian.

APPENDIX.

Arrivals of Steamboats at Fort Union, and later at Fort Buford, 1864-69, as noted in Larpenteur's Orig. Journs. (With some data for Fort Benton during these years, from Cont. Mont. Hist. Soc., and various additional items.)

1864.

May 31. *Benton* arr. 5 a. m., bringing Larpenteur to his post. She arr. Benton June 10; again June 27, tripping from Milk r.; arr. mouth Maria's r. July 9, tripping from Milk r.

June 10. *Fanny Ogden* arr. noon, bound up. She brought Maj. Wilkinson and his clerk, with annuities for Assiniboines and Crows. No Benton record.

" 13. *Yellowstone* arr. 10.30 a. m., bound up. Brought a part of Capt. Greer's company. Left 3 p. m., with Maj. Upton. Reached Cow isl. June 21.

" 17. *Fanny Ogden* arr. soon after sunrise; left in an hour, bound down.

" 17. *Welcome* arr. as *Fanny Ogden* left. Brought rest of Capt. Greer's company and balance of Indian annuities. Left next day, bound up to Galpin.

" 17. *Benton* arr. ½ hour after *Welcome*. Left before sunset, bound up.

" 18. *Cutter* arr. 5 a. m. Left next morning, bound up. She reached Benton July 14.

" 23. *Welcome* arr. before sunrise from Galpin. Left same day, bound down, with Maj. Wilkinson and some annuities which had been brought up to Union by mistake.

1864.

June 24. *Effie Deans*, Capt. John Labarge, arr. 4 p. m. Discharged next day. Left 26th, bound up. Reached Maria's r. July 9.

July 5. *Yellowstone* arr. from Cow isl. Left next day, bound down.

"   16. *Effie Deans* arr. from Maria's r. Left same day, bound down.

"   23. *Benton* arr. from Maria's r. Left 27th for St. Louis.

"   25. *Belle Peoria* arr. from below. Discharged, and left Aug. 2 for St. Louis.

"   25. *Chippewa Falls* arr. from below. Left Aug. 2 for Brazeau's house on Yellowstone r.

"   25. *Alone* arr. from below. Left Aug. 2 for Brazeau's house on Yellowstone r.

"   25. *General Grant* arr. from below. Left Aug. 1 for Fort Rice.

"   25. *Island City*, Capt. Alex. Lamont, master, Capt. John Gillam, pilot, was to arr., but snagged 8 miles below; total wreck; no lives lost. The 4 other boats which arr. 25th went to her assistance; were wrecking several days.

Aug. 13. *General Grant* arr. 5 p. m. from Fort Rice. Brought news of Sully's Sioux campaign. Left 10.30 a. m. next day, bound down.

"   17. *Chippewa Falls* arr. p. m. from Five isls. on the Yellowstone. *Alone* expected next day. No record of her arrival, or of departure of either of these boats.

1865.

May 19. *Yellowstone* arr. 2 p. m., with a company of soldiers from Fort Rice. Left 5 p. m., bound up. Reached Benton before June 1.

"   20. *Deer Lodge* arr. 10.30 p. m. Left next daybreak, bound up. Reached Benton before June 1; also, twice in June, tripping; also, Dauphin rapids, July 21.

1865.

May 27. *Benton* arr. 11 a. m. Left 3 p. m., bound up. No record of reaching Benton.

June 1. *Effie Deans* arr. 5 a. m. Left same day, bound up. Reached Maria's r. in June.

" 1. *St. John* arr. 5. a. m. Left same day, after funeral of a child who had died on board, bound up. Reached Maria's r. June 25.

" 3. *General Grant* arr. sunset. No further record.

" 5. *Yellowstone* arr. 1.30 p. m. from Benton. Left next sunrise, bound down.

" 6. *Kate Kearney* arr. sunset. Left 19th, bound up. No Benton record.

" 10. *Lillie Martin* arr. Left next day, bound up. No Benton record.

" 11. *Twilight* arr. a. m., after lightening by discharging part of freight 2 m. below. Left at noon. Reached Maria's r. June 29.

" 13. *Benton* arr. from above. Left early next day, bound down.

" 17. *Oronoacke* [*sic*] sighted early a. m., did not get over bar till late p. m. Brought news that Jeff. Davis had been hanged (!), and that Chouteau had sold out to Hubble, Hawley and Co., now styled the N. W. Co. Left next day, bound up. No Benton record.

" 18. *Fanny Ogden* arr. p. m. Left same day, bound up. No Benton record.

" 21. *David Watts* arr. Left 27th, bound up.

" 23. *Hattie May* sighted; could not get over bar till next day. Left 25th or 26th, bound up.

" 23. *Cutter* arr. from above (last record was at Benton July 14, 1864.) Left 3 p. m. next day, with 100,000 rations for Fort Berthold.

" 25. *St. John* arr. from Maria's r.

" 26. *Sam Gaty,* new, arr. from below. Left next day, bound up.

1865.

June 26. *Benton* arr. from below. Left next day, bound up.

" 26. *General Grant* arr. from below. Left next day, bound up.

" 26. *Kate Kearney* arr. from above. Discharged 623 sacks of flour. Left next day for St. Louis.

July 5. *Hattie May* arr. from a point 12 m. above Milk r., where they had made a place called Fort Kaiser to store goods, near Fort Copland (or Copelin ?), which was built for the same purpose. Left same day, bound up.

" 6. *Benton* arr. early a. m. from above. Left same day at 11 a. m. for Fort Copland.

" 6. *Fanny Ogden* arr. 7 a. m. from above and left immediately, bound down.

" 9. *Twilight* arr. 10 a. m. from Maria's r. Left 11 a. m. for St. Louis, taking 2 tons of freight for Fort Berthold. (Larpenteur on 11th again says *Twilight* left that day, either by error of ,date or by giving a wrong name.)

" 11. *Hattie May* arr. sunset from above Milk r. and left for St. Louis.

" 11. *Lillie Martin* arr. 11 a. m. from above. Left same day, bound down.

" 13. *Benton* arr. from Fort Copland. Left p. m. for St. Louis: but see July 21.

" 14. *Prairie State* arr. 10 a. m. from below. Discharged freight. Left 11 a. m. July 20, bound up.

" 14. *Converse* arr. a. m. from below and left immediately, bound up.

" 17. *Effie Deans* arr. early a. m. from Maria's r. Left early a. m. next day, bound down.

" 19. *Oronoacke* arr. from above. Left same day, bound down.

" 19. *David Watts* arr. from above. Left same day, bound down.

1865.

July 21. *Benton* arr. early a. m., having met the *Graham* at the Tobacco Garden and brought up part of latter's freight; the *Oronoacke* to bring up the balance of it. The *Benton* having discharged, and taken on about 600 sacks of bacon of the *Sam Gaty's* freight, left for Fort Copland 2 p. m., July 23.

" 22. *Deer Lodge* arr. this p. m. or 23d p. m. from above. Left 24th for Fort Copland.

" 23. *Fanny Ogden* arr. p. m. from below. Left early a. m. 24th for St. Louis. She brought Dr. Washington Matthews, U. S. A.

" 24. *General Grant* arr. early a. m. from above, with orders to take on all freight left by the *Benton* and return to Fort Copland. Left early next day.

" 26. *General Grant* arr. again, having run aground and been ordered back to Union to unload, then to return empty to assist other boats above. She discharged, and left 5 p. m. next day.

" 28. *Deer Lodge* and *Benton* arr. 10 a. m. from above, with orders to discharge and go below to help other boats up. Both left next day, 10 and 7 a. m.

Aug. 3. *General Grant* arr. sunset from above. Left 3.30 p. m. next day for Copland.

" 4. *Benton* arr. from vicinity of Berthold, bringing balance of *Graham's* freight, consisting of machinery; discharged 2 m. below Union, and started back 5 p. m.

" 12. *General Grant* arr. 10.30 a. m. from above, and began to load to return to Copland. Next day express arr. from Berthold with orders from Gen. Sully for Capt. Upton's Co. B to come down. So the *Grant* was unloaded, pressed into this service, and left for Berthold 1.30 p. m., 14th, with about 80 soldiers on board.

" 17. *Big Horn* arr. 3 p. m. from below, empty, to take down commissioners and soldiers. Left 5 p. m., 21st;

Government affairs ended at Union; Larpenteur
left in charge, with Clerk Herrick, Mr. C. Conklin,
and 6 working men. (This boat, or one of the same
name, stern-wheeler, 178 x 31 ft., was wrecked 8 m.
below Poplar r., in the 2d bend, May 8, 1883.)

1865.

Aug. 23. *General Grant* arr. from Berthold, bound up to Copland; gave up this trip; loaded Government stores,
and left 31st, bound down. (She was wrecked in ice
next year, Mar. 18, 1866, 3 m. below Bellevue, Neb.,
having on board 172 tons of freight for Benton)

Sept. 15. *Converse* arr. 3 p. m. from above. Left 2 p. m. next
day, bound down.

"   17. *Hattie May* arr. 8 p. m., bringing up members of the
N. W. Co. Left 11.30 a. m. next day, bound down.
Last boat up to Union this year.

1866.   Larpenteur did not reach Union (Buford) till June 11,
when he came on the *Sunset* and his record begins.
Mont. Hist. Soc. list of arrivals of boats at Benton,
May and June, is: *St. John*, May 18; *Deer Lodge*,
18th; *Cora*, 20th; *Waverly*, 22d; *W. J. Lewis*, 31st;
Mollie Dozier, June 1; *Marcella*, 5th; *Ontario*, 5th;
Big Horn, 6th; *Walter B. Dance*, 8th; *Iron City*,
9th; *Amelia Poe*, 11th; *Peter Balen*, 11th—seven
boats here at one time; *Miner*, 13th; *Only Chance*,
13th; *Tacony*, 15th; *Favorite*, 15th; *Gold Finch*, 15th;
Luella, 17th; *Helena*, 27th; *Tom Stevens*, 28th;
David Watts, 29th; *Lillie Martin*, 29th; *Agnes*, 30th.
Consequently all these boats had arr. at Union (Buford) before Larpenteur's record begins, as follows:

June 11. *Sunset* arr. 5 a. m. from below. Left 7 a. m., bound
up. She arr. Benton July 1.

"   11. *Ontario* arr. from Benton, bound down.

"   12. *Mary McDonald* arr. from below. Dropped down to
old Fort William to discharge for Buford.

1866.

June 12. *Huntsville* arr. from below, bound up.   She arr. Benton July 4.

"   14. *Big Horn* arr. 10 a. m. from Benton, bound down.

"   14. *Agnes* arr. noon, bound up.   She arr. Benton June 30.

"   16. *Walter B. Dance* arr. from Benton.

"   17. *Iron City* arr. from Benton, bound down: see next.

"   18. *Iron City*, from Benton, passed without stopping. (Probable error in this duplication of a name.)

"   19. *Only Chance* arr. 3 p. m. from Benton.   Windbound till next day; left very early, bound down.

"   21. *Big Horn* arr. late p. m. from below, bringing 2 companies of soldiers from Benton.   Left early next a. m.   No Benton record of arrival this trip.

"   21. *Peter Balen* arr. late p. m. from Benton.   Left early next a. m., bound down.

"   22. *Tacony* arr. from Benton.

"   23. *Gold Finch* arr. from Benton.

"   23. *Gallatin* arr. 1 p. m. from below.   Left immediately, bound up.   She arr. Benton July 19—last boat up there this year.

"   25. *Marion* arr. early a. m., 75 days out from St. Louis. Left next day.   She arr. Benton July 13.   Wrecked on her return trip at Assiniboine Ldg.   Stern-wheeler, Capt. Wm. Shanks, master.

"   25. *Waverly* at old Fort William Ldg. this p. m.

"   25. *Cora* at old Fort William Ldg. this p. m.

"   25. *Rubicon* at old Fort William Ldg. this p. m., "being the flagboat of the fleet of which General Reeves is the commander."   The fleet of 4 boats passed by next p. m.

"   26. *Miner* arr. from Benton.   Left next day, 1 p. m.

"   28. *Luella* arr. from Benton, to take freight hence to Benton.   Left next day 6 a. m.   On this 2d trip she arr. Benton July 11.

1866.

June 29. *Nellie Rogers* arr. 7 p. m. from below, took on a little ice and left at once. She arr. Benton July 12.

July 3. *Montana* arr. from above (no Benton record for her. Larpenteur says she "returned" with the *Helena*). Left same day.

" 3. *Helena* arr. from Benton, and remained. Departure not noted.

" 3. *Rubicon* arr. from above (no Benton record for her). Left same day. These 3 boats brought news of killing of mate of the *Iron City* by Indians; her whereabouts uncertain: see above, June 17 and 18. But the mate recovered from his wounds.

" 4. *Deer Lodge* arr. last night from St. Louis; transport, bound up on her 2d round trip this year. Departure not noted. She arr. Benton July 13 (her 1st arrival having been May 18, as above; her 1st down trip past Buford not given).

" 4. *Ontario* arr. last night from Fort Sully; transport. She reported Peace Commissioners' boat near Berthold, coming up slowly. Departure not noted; no Benton record on this trip.

" 5. *Lillie Martin* arr. 9 a. m. from Benton. Left at once, bound down.

" 7. *David Watts* arr. after sunset from Benton. Departure not noted.

" 8. *Sunset* arr. 9 a. m. from Benton. Left same day for the States.

" 9. *Agnes* arr. from Benton with 150 passengers. Left at sunset, bound down.

" 10. *Ben Johnson* arr. 10 a. m. from below; Peace Commissioners' boat. Left next day at noon "on a hunt up the Missouri." Returned 13th; left 17th; went 2 miles up; returned 18th. Left for St. Louis 19th, 4 p. m.

1866.

July 14. *Huntsville* arr. from Benton, with 5 following transports from above:

" 14. *Iron City* arr. from above. ⎫
" 14. *Cora* arr. from above. ⎪
" 14. *St. John* arr. from above. ⎬ Departures not noted.
" 14. *Big Horn* arr. from above. ⎪
" 14. *Ontario* arr. from above. ⎭

" 15. *Amanda* arr. 10 a. m. from below, with Crow annities. Left 17th, sunset, for Judith r.

" 18. *Deer Lodge* arr. from above (recorded at Benton July 13. Larpenteur says she arr. from Judith r.). Departure not noted.

" 19. *Nellie Rogers* arr. from Benton. This day, as noted above, the *Ben Johnson* finally left for St. Louis, and Larpenteur went on her. At date of 27th, his Journ. states, at Fort Berthold, that the *Waverly, Mary McKelon* (?) and *Amanda* returned from above— the former from near Judith r., "where soldiers have made their selection for building a military post," no doubt meaning Fort Claggett.

1867. Larpenteur did not reach Union (Buford) till June 19, when he came on the *Jennie Brown*, and his record begins. Mont. Hist. Soc. list of 24 arrivals of boats at Benton, to July 6, when the *Jennie* arr. there, is: *Waverly* and *Miner*, in May; *Only Chance*, June 1; *Deer Lodge*, June 3; *Walter B. Dance*, June 3; *Gallatin*, June 7; *Amelia Poe*, June 9; *Mountaineer*, June 10; *St. John*, June 10; *Yorktown*, June 11; *Nile*, June 12; *Ben Johnson*, June 13; *Huntsville*, June 14; *Ida Stockdale*, June 16; *Octavia*, June 20; *Guidon*, June 20; *Benton*, June 26; *Ida Stockdale*, June 29; *Amaranth*, June 29; *G. A. Thompson*, July 1; *Antelope*, July 3; *Abeona*, July 4; *Agnes*, July 5; *Tacony*, July 5. Consequently, all these boats had arr. at Union and Buford before Larpenteur's record begins, as follows:

1867.

June 19. *Jennie Brown* arr. 2.30 a. m., left 7 a. m. She arr. Benton July 6.

" 23. *Viola Belle* arr. a. m., bound up. She arr. Benton July 23.

" 26. *Lillie* arr. Buford from the States. Passed Union 27th. She arr. Benton July 12.

" 26. *Ben Johnson* arr. 6 p. m. from Benton. Left same day, bound down.

" 27. *Lady Grace* arr. Buford from below; discharged 80 tons freight. Passed Union early next a. m. She arr. Benton July 11.

" 28. *Octavia* arr. noon from Benton, bound down. Departure not noted.

" 28. *Ida Fulton* passed up 2 p. m. She arr. Benton July 16.

" 28. *Graham* arr. Buford 6 p. m., bringing Commissioners and Father De Smet. Started back for the States early next a. m.

July 1. *Benton* arr. from Benton, bound down. Departure not noted.

" 1. *Paragon* arr. Buford with Government goods. Went no further.

" 3. *Silver Lake* arr. Buford. Passed Union 4th, bound up. No Benton record.

" 4. *Ida Stockdale* arr. from Benton. She brought some of the machinery of the *Trover*, which had grounded and been abandoned at Trover or Franchette Point; stern-wheeler, 160 x 32 ft.

" 5. *City of Pekin* arr. Buford from below. Government boat, going no further. Departure not noted.

" 6. *G. A.* or ("*J. A.*") *Thompson* arr. from Benton, bound down. Departure not noted.

" 6. *Amaranth* arr. from Benton, bound down. Departure not noted.

" 8. *Richmond* arr. a. m., bound up. She arr. Benton July 28.

1867.

July 11. *Jennie Brown* arr. from Benton. Left same day, bound down.

" 11. *Abeona* arr. from Benton, bound down.

" 11. *Agnes* arr. late p. m. from Benton, bound down.

" 13. *Tacony* arr. from Benton, bound down.

" 15. *Big Horn* arr. from Benton, where she had arr. July 8.

" 16. *Imperial* arr. Buford, bound up. Left next day, taking men to wreck the *Trover*. She only reached Cow isl., date not given.

" 16. *Ida Stockdale* arr., having on board Gen. Terry, en route to Helena, Mont. Left next p. m.

" 18. *Lady Grace* arr. early a. m. from Benton.

" 20. *Lillie* arr. from Benton, bringing 20 Crows whom Gen. Sully had sent for by Thos. Campbell and Louis Bompart.

" 22. *Tom Stevens* arr. from Benton, where she had arr. July 10. Left for Milk r. 25th, on Government service, taking a lot of Crows and Assiniboines.

" 22. *Ida Fulton* arr. from Benton.

" 23. *Sunset* arr. from Omaha, bound for Benton. No Benton record.

" 23. *Little Rock* arr. from Benton, where she had arr. July 14.

" 31. *Nymph* arr. from Benton, where she had arr. July 20; reported up boats aground. This is *Nymph No. 2* of Benton record for 1867. She was a stern-wheeler, wrecked next year, Mar. 3, 1868, on chain of rocks at Sibley bridge, Mo.

Aug. 3. *Miner* arr. Buford; arr. Union next day; left 1 p. m., "having demolished the old Union kitchen for fire-wood." Apparently her 2d trip up this year, as she is reported at Benton in May. No 2d arrival at Benton recorded. Said to have got up to Cow isl.

" 5. *Ida Stockdale* arr. from Benton, bound down.

" 6. *Only Chance* arr. Buford, bound up. She arr. Benton Aug. 29.

1867.

Aug. 7. *Centralia* arr., bound up. ' No Benton record.

" 7. *Carrie* arr. Buford. Government boat; her 2d trip. Went no further. Departure not noted.

" 8. *Viola Belle* arr. from Benton, bound down. She was a side-wheeler, valued at $15,000; snagged on Smith's Bar, Doniphan Bend, Aug. 27, 1871; boat and cargo total loss.

" 11. *Huntsville* arr. Buford and passed Union 4 p. m., bound for Benton. She only reached Cow isl.

" 12. *Luella* arr. from Benton, where she had arr. July 8. Bound down, with 200 passengers.

" 17. *Guidon* arr. from Benton, bound down; Gen. Alfred H. Terry and staff on board.

" 19. *Richmond* arr. early a. m. from Benton, bound down; could not make a landing, and went on.

" 24. *Deer Lodge* arr. a. m. Buford; went 5 miles up Yellowstone r. to wood and returned. Left next a. m. for St. Louis.

" 27. *Miner* arr. from Cow isl., reporting that none of the late boats could get up to Benton.

" 27. *Last Chance* arr. Buford with Indian annuities. Went no further.

" 28. *Tom Stevens* arr. from above.

" 29. *Centralia* arr. from Fort Hawley, not having been able to get any further up. She had discharged Government freight at Fort Peck.

Sept. 21. *Only Chance* arr. early a. m. from Benton, with about 200 passengers, bound down.

" 26. *Huntsville* arr. from Cow isl., full of passengers, bound down.

Oct. 6. *Gallatin* arr. from above in bad shape, guards all gone, etc.; had been reported a wreck, but got off. She was a stern-wheeler, 140 x 30 feet, finally wrecked next year, Apr. 16, 1868, at Little Sioux r.

1867.

Oct. 18. *Imperial* arr. from Cow isl. with nearly 300 passengers, bound down.

" 25. *Zephyr* arr. Buford after sunset, from above. Her up trip this year is not noted by Larpenteur. Benton record for Sept. 6, 1867. A boat of this name, probably same boat, built for Arkansaw river trade, owned by Ben Johnson, running irregularly on the Missouri, was wrecked near Sibley, Mo., about 1875.

" 26. *Amaranth* arr. from below, with 1500 bushels corn. Went no further.

" 31. *Benton* arr. late p. m. from below; Durfee and Peck's boat, with " the largest equipment ever brought to this post." Last boat up. Left next day at noon.

1868.   Larpenteur was at his post on the opening of the season, and his record begins with the first boat up.

Apr. 26. *Cora* passed up 3 p. m. without stopping. She arr. Benton May 15.

" 30. *Success* arr. at dusk. She arr. Benton May 15.

" 30. *Deer Lodge* arr. at sunset. Left late May 2. She arr. Benton May 19.

May 1. *Nile* arr. late. Left next day. She arr. Benton May 21.

" 10. *Only Chance* arr., 45 days out. She arr. Benton May 25.

" 12. *Sallie* arr. 6 p. m. She arr. Benton May 25.

" 13. *St. Luke* arr. noon, and went on. She arr. Benton May 28.

" 13. *Miner* arr. noon. Left at daylight 15th. She arr. Benton May 25.

" 18. *Henry Adkins* arr. noon. Discharged some freight for Buford and went on. She arr. Benton May 30.

" 18. *Antelope* arr. noon. Discharged for Buford and went on. She arr. Benton June 1.

" 19. *Mountaineer* arr. 2 a. m. She arr. Benton May 30.

" 19. *Huntsville* arr. 5 a. m. She arr. Benton June 1.

" 19. *Peninah* arr. 4 p. m. She arr. Benton May 31.

" 19. *Octavia* arr. 4 p. m. She arr. Benton May 31.

1868.

May 19. *Ida Stockdale* arr. 5 p. m. She arr. Benton May 31.

"   20. *Amelia Poe* passed 6 p. m. without stopping; wrecked on this trip, 23d, about 5 m. below Little Porcupine r., directly opposite present Lenox sta. of the G. N. Ry. She was a stern-wheeler of 327 tons, 175 x 30 feet, owned by Capt. Wm. Poe and named for his wife; Capt. Thomas Townsend, master at the time. Boat total loss; most of cargo saved. Some quartz-mill machinery left on the bank is there now (1898).

"   21. *Bertha* arr. 6 p. m. She arr. Benton June 2.

"   26. *Guidon* arr. late. Left early next day. She arr. Benton June 8.

"   26. *Lacon* arr. late. Left early next day. She arr. Benton June 8.

"   28. *Cora* arr. from Benton, and went on down at once.

"   31. *Yorktown* arr. 7.30 a. m. She arr. Benton June 14.

"   31. *Only Chance* arr. 1 p. m. from Benton, and went on down.

"   31. *Success* arr. 6 p. m. from Benton, and went on down.

June 1. *Hiram Woods* arr. from below. She arr. Benton June 23.

"   1. *Deer Lodge* arr. from Benton, and went on down.

"   2. *Sallie* arr. from Benton and went on down.

"   3. *Benton* arr. from below; army paymaster on board. She arr. Benton June 13.

"   3. *Ida Reese* arr. from below. She arr. Benton June 16.

"   3. *Fanny Barker* arr. from below. She arr. Benton June 20.

"   3. *North Alabama* arr. from below. She arr. Benton June 20.

"   3. *Andrew Ackley* arr. from below. She arr. Benton June 17.

"   3. *St. Luke* arr. from Benton and went on down.

"   3. *Miner* arr. from Benton and went on down.

"   4. *Nile* arr. 7 a. m. from Benton and went on down.

"   6. *Columbia* arr. from below. She arr. Benton June 27.

"   7. *Urilda* arr. from below. She arr. Benton June 28.

1868.

June 7. *Henry Adkins* arr. from Benton a little before sunset. Larpenteur took passage on her and went 15 miles down. His record ends here.

Benton records later this season are: *Importer*, June 15; *Viola Belle*, 26th; *Deer Lodge*, July 4; *Tom Stevens*, 7th; *Silver Lake No. 4*, 7th; *Andrew Ackley*, 23d; *Leni Leoti*, 26th; *Success*, Aug. 4. The *Andrew Ackley* also brought up some boat's freight in Aug. from Dauphin rapids, and cleared from Benton for St. Louis Aug. 27.

1869. Larpenteur's record begins with the first boat up.

May 4. *Deer Lodge* arr. early from below and left in 15 minutes. She arr. Benton 19th.

" 17. *Importer* arr. 8 a. m. from below. She arr. Benton 27th.

" 17. *Nile* arr. 1 p. m. from below. She arr. Benton 27th.

" 17. *Cora* arr. 7 p. m. from below. She arr. Benton 31st.

" 18. *Fanny Barker* arr. 7 p. m. from below. Gen. P. R. De Trobriand on board, en route for Fort Shaw, on Sun r. She arr. Benton June 1.

" 19. *Ida Reese No. 2* arr. 10 a. m. from below. She arr. Benton 30th.

" 19. *North Alabama* arr. 2 p. m. from below; discharged some freight. She arr. Benton June 4.

" 21. *Silver Bow* arr. 6 a. m. from below. She arr. Benton June 4.

" 22. *Peninah* passed, bound up; did not stop. She arr. Benton June 8.

" 23. *Big Horn* passed, bound up; did not stop. She arr. Benton June 8.

" 24. *Huntsville* arr. from below. She arr. Benton June 11.

" 24. *Lacon* arr. from below; discharged some Government freight. She arr. Benton June 15.

" 26. *Deer Lodge* arr. from Benton, loaded with passengers; 90 or more for this place.

" 31. *Colossal* arr. 7 a. m. from below to-day (or June 1). She arr. Benton June 20.

1869.

May 31. *Peter Balen* arr. 10 a. m. from below. She arr. Benton June 18.

" 31. *Mollie Herbert* arr. 10 a. m. No Benton record.

June 1. *Silver Lake No. 4* arr. 11 a. m. She arr. Benton June 16.

" 1. *Arkansas* arr. 3 a. m. No Benton record.

" 2. *Utah* arr. at sunset. She arr. Benton June 15.

" 2. *Bertha* arr. about dark. She arr. Benton June 21.

Larpenteur's record ends here. It does not name the following 7 boats, which have Benton records for June this year: *Andrew Ackley*, 8th; *Only Chance*, 8th; *Viola Belle*, 10th; *Sallie*, 11th; *Mountaineer*, 11th; *H. M. Shreve*, 12th; *Miner*, 14th—all of which presumably passed Buford, bound up.

Besides these, the following boats arr. at Benton, double-tripping from Dauphin rapids: *Cora*, June 5; *Silver Bow*, 8th; *North Alabama*, with part of *Mountaineer's* freight, 9th; *Big Horn*, 13th; *North Alabama*, with part of *H. M. Shreve's* freight, 13th; *Only Chance*, 14th; *Fanny Barker*, 14th; *Viola Belle*, 14th; *Peninah*, 14th; *Andrew Ackley*, 15th; *Huntsville*, 19th; *Big Horn*, 20th; *Miner*, 21st; *Peninah*, 23d; *Only Chance*, 23d; *Silver Lake*, 24th; *Peter Balen*, 26th; *Andrew Ackley*, July 2.

NOTE.—Before 1864 the only "Benton boats" were: 1859, *Chippewa* reached Fort Brulé, 6 m. above Maria's r., 16 m. below Benton, July 17.— 1860, *Chippewa* and *Key West*, both at Benton, July 2; the first boats that ever reached that place. —1861, none, the *Chippewa* having burned at Disaster Bend June 23, 1861, as narrated by Larpenteur, p. 326.—1862, *Emilie* and *Shreveport*, June 17; *Key West No. 2* and *Spread Eagle*, June 20.— 1863, *Shreveport* to Cow isl., 123 m. by land from Benton, June 20; *Alone*, to Milk r. only; date unknown.

INDEX.

O

P

THE END.

DR. COUES' WORKS ON WESTERN EXPLORATION.

Expeditions of Zebulon Montgomery Pike.

To the Headwaters of the Mississippi River, the Interior Parts of Louisiana, Mexico and Texas, in the years of 1805-6-7. Reprinted in full from the original Philadelphia edition of 1810. With copious explanatory, geographical and scientific notes to the text, a new Memoir of Pike and an Index to the whole. By Prof. Elliott Coues, Edition limited, 3 vols., 8vo.

1,000 on fine book paper	$10.00 net per set.
150 on hand-made paper	$20.00 net per set.

This edition of Pike's explorations is only second in value to the annotated journals of Lewis & Clark, by the same editor. The rearrangement by Dr. Coues of the appendices and other extraneous matter adds very greatly to its value, since in the original edition even the experienced reader has found it difficult to collate complete information on many important topics. The volumes are an important contribution to geographical and historical literature.—*The Nation* (3 columns).

On the whole, the new Pike must prove monumental. It will forever link its author with Pike's fame. Its map of Mississippi sources, and the arduous voyage (of the editor) into the farthest fountains, will not let us wonder that the Minnesota Park Commissioner styled a lakelet feeding Itasca, Elliott Coues, and inscribed that name upon a boulder on that utmost shore.—*American Historical Review* (2½ pages).

The great merit in Dr. Coues' notes is that they preserve the history of the localities and give credit to all the local historians and archæologists. Dr. Coues seems to have read all of the local histories and records, whether contained in books, pamphlets or even newspapers, and has given the references with great painstaking. In fact, the notes are equivalent to a bibliography.—*American Antiquarian and Oriental Journal.*

Dr. Coues' new edition of "Pike's Expeditions" is a beautiful specimen of presswork most creditable to the taste and liberality of the publisher. The editor has done the material portion of his work as successfully as has the publisher, the result is a well-digested and most readable chronicle, instead of ill-assorted bundles of information (as in the original edition). No explorer has ever been more fully aided to express himself through the ampler knowledges of the generations that come after him than in this case.—*The Dial* (2½ pages).

New Light on the Early History of the Greater Northwest.

The Journals of Alexander Henry (Partner of the Northwest Company), with Explorations and Life with the Fur Traders on the Red, Saskatchewan, and Columbia Rivers, 1799-1814, now first published, with which are collated the original unpublished manuscripts of David Thompson, Explorer and Geographer of the Northwest Company. The whole carefully edited with copious notes by Dr. Elliott Coues, with Maps, Index, etc. Limited edition, 3 vols., roy. 8vo, 1,000 copies, fine book paper $10.00 net per set.
100 on hand-made paper $20.00 net per set.

Dr. Coues says of this work: "No work approaching these journals in the scope, extent, variety and interest of its contents has appeared since the publication in 1801 of Sir Alexander Mackenzie's memorable voyages, and the present work will undoubtedly take rank with that classic as a veritable mine of accurate information." Send for complete prospectus.

"The exceeding value of the work lies in the fact that it is new. Not for a long time has a book of such great historical interest been published in this country * * * it should become a cherished book in the eyes of all those who take more than a passing interest in the early history of our country."—*New York Herald.*

"The claim of the publisher that few such important books as this have been issued recently, is a just one. The work is all that could be desired in every way."—*Cincinnati Commercial-Tribune.*

"He (Dr. Coues) beheld in Henry that which he most desired to complete his magnificent endeavor to illuminate the world of the West during the early years of the nineteenth century."—*The Nation.*

"Dr. Coues study and research as shown in these volumes is simply marvelous."—*New York Tribune.*

"It will be seen also that Henry and Thompson to a degree overlap Lewis and Clark."—*The Dial.*

"The study of the Indians was his (Henry's) life work. Here he is keenest and most valuable."—*Baltimore Sun.*